RULED BY LOVE

Another *aide-de-camp*, even older than the one who had first escorted them into the Palace, announced,

"His Royal Highness is ready to receive his guests."

Zoleka walked towards the door.

They had to cross a passage and into another room where Prince Majmir was waiting.

She was uncertain as what she expected him to look like, but she was not at all prepared for the rather decrepit man who was waiting in the centre of the room to receive them.

His evening clothes did not seem to fit him and his hair, which was slightly grey, was unkempt.

Even before she reached him, Zoleka's instinct told her there was something very wrong.

However, she swept dutifully to the floor into a low curtsy and Prince Majmir bowed to her.

"Welcome to Krnov. I very much hope Your Royal Highness will enjoy being here with us."

"I am certain I shall. It is exceedingly gracious of Your Royal Highness to invite me to your Palace and I am delighted to be your guest."

THE BARBARA CARTLAND PINK COLLECTION

Titles in this series

RULED BY LOVE

BARBARA CARTLAND

Barbaracartland.com Ltd

THE BARBARA CARTLAND PINK COLLECTION

Barbara Cartland was the most prolific bestselling author in the history of the world. She was frequently in the Guinness Book of Records for writing more books in a year than any other living author. In fact her most amazing literary feat was when her publishers asked for more Barbara Cartland romances, she doubled her output from 10 books a year to over 20 books a year, when she was 77.

She went on writing continuously at this rate for 20 years and wrote her last book at the age of 97, thus completing 400 books between the ages of 77 and 97.

Her publishers finally could not keep up with this phenomenal output, so at her death she left 160 unpublished manuscripts, something again that no other author has ever achieved.

Now the exciting news is that these 160 original unpublished Barbara Cartland books are already being published and by Barbaracartland.com exclusively on the internet, as the international web is the best possible way of reaching so many Barbara Cartland readers around the world.

The 160 books are published monthly and will be numbered in sequence.

The series is called the Pink Collection as a tribute to Barbara Cartland whose favourite colour was pink and it became very much her trademark over the years.

The Barbara Cartland Pink Collection is published only on the internet. Log on to www.barbaracartland.com to find out how you can purchase the books monthly as they are published, and take out a subscription that will ensure that all subsequent editions are delivered to you by mail order to your home.

NEW

Barbaracartland.com is proud to announce the publication of ten new Audio Books for the first time as CDs. They are favourite Barbara Cartland stories read by well-known actors and actresses and each story extends to 4 or 5 CDs. The Audio Books are as follows:

The Patient Bridegroom	The Passion and the Flower
A Challenge of Hearts	Little White Doves of Love
A Train to Love	The Prince and the Pekinese
The Unbroken Dream	A King in Love
The Cruel Count	A Sign of Love

More Audio Books will be published in the future and the above titles can be purchased by logging on to the website www.barbaracartland.com or please write to the address below.

If you do not have access to a computer, you can write for information about the Barbara Cartland Pink Collection and the Barbara Cartland Audio Books to the following address:

Barbara Cartland.com Ltd., Camfield Place,
Hatfield, Hertfordshire AL9 6JE, United Kingdom.

Telephone: +44 (0)1707 642629
Fax: +44 (0)1707 663041

THE LATE DAME BARBARA CARTLAND

Barbara Cartland who sadly died in May 2000 at the age of nearly 99 was the world's most famous romantic novelist who wrote 723 books in her lifetime with worldwide sales of over 1 billion copies and her books were translated into 36 different languages.

As well as romantic novels, she wrote historical biographies, 6 autobiographies, theatrical plays, books of advice on life, love, vitamins and cookery. She also found time to be a political speaker and television and radio personality.

She wrote her first book at the age of 21 and this was called *Jigsaw*. It became an immediate bestseller and sold 100,000 copies in hardback and was translated into 6 different languages. She wrote continuously throughout her life, writing bestsellers for an astonishing 76 years. Her books have always been immensely popular in the United States, where in 1976 her current books were at numbers 1 & 2 in the B. Dalton bestsellers list, a feat never achieved before or since by any author.

Barbara Cartland became a legend in her own lifetime and will be best remembered for her wonderful romantic novels, so loved by her millions of readers throughout the world.

Her books will always be treasured for their moral message, her pure and innocent heroines, her good looking and dashing heroes and above all her belief that the power of love is more important than anything else in everyone's life.

"'I love you' are the easiest words to say in any language, but in reality they are the hardest words to really mean from the heart."

Barbara Cartland

CHAPTER ONE
1820

Princess Zoleka of Opava dismounted, thanked her groom for his attendance and walked into the Palace.

An *aide-de-camp* came towards her and she asked,

"Where is His Royal Highness?"

"In the library, Your Royal Highness," he replied.

She ran speedily through the corridors of the vast Royal Palace to the library, where she knew that her father would be concentrating on the book he was writing.

It was a History of Silesia and it was undoubtedly going to take him a long time.

When she opened the door, he looked up and when he saw who it was, he smiled.

"You are back, Zoleka, I see."

"I am back, Papa, and the new stallion is splendid. He gallops very much faster than all the others, so you and I must have a race one day."

Prince Lászlé smiled at his beautiful daughter.

"I will try and manage it tomorrow if I am not too busy."

He rose from the writing desk as he was speaking and walked across the room.

"I want to talk to you, Zoleka."

As he spoke seriously she looked at him in surprise.

He was a very handsome man and although his hair had a touch of grey in it, he still had an active and athletic body.

He was, his daughter was the first to recognise, a magnificent rider.

Prince Lászlé stood in front of the fireplace which, as it was high summer, was filled with fragrant flowers, while Zoleka sat down on the sofa and waited.

She knew only too well that when her father took up this particular position, he had something serious to say.

When he did not speak, she asked,

"What is it, Papa?"

"It is something I am afraid you will not like, but it is something you may have to do."

"*Have to do?*" echoed Zoleka.

She was wondering what it could possibly be.

"There arrived this morning," her father continued, "a messenger from the Prime Minister of Krnov."

"From Krnov!" exclaimed Zoleka. "Whatever did he want?"

"He wants – you to travel to Krnov to take up the position of Lady-in-Waiting to Princess Udele."

"Lady-in-Waiting! I hope you said 'no'."

"As a matter of fact, I asked for time to discuss it with you, because I do not really think that 'no' is the right answer at this particular time."

"But, Papa, of course I don't want to go away from you and live in Krnov. Why should I? And I believe you would miss me."

"Of course I would miss you," her father answered. "My instinct was the same as yours, to say 'no' at once."

"Why did you not do so, Papa?"

"When I talked to the envoy who had been sent by the Prime Minister, I realised that the situation in Krnov is rather more serious than I had previously thought."

"What situation and what is serious?"

"You should know as well as I do, my dear Zoleka, that Opava, Krnov and Cieszyn are all that are left of what was once a free Silesia."

Zoleka was well aware of this situation.

She had been told so often how under the Treaty of Berlin in 1742, Queen Maria Theresa of Austria had been forced to cede Upper and Lower Silesia to King Frederick II of Prussia.

The only exceptions to the Treaty were the three small Principalities of Krnov, Opava and Cieszyn.

In the Seven Years War which began fourteen years later and lasted until 1763, the Austrians had attempted to recover Silesia but without avail.

At one time Silesia had been comprised of sixteen Principalities running their own lives, each under its own Ruler.

In the usual domineering manner of the Prussians, Frederick II had coerced most of them into becoming part of his Kingdom.

The real reason why the Prussians were so keen to have and keep Upper Silesia was the rising importance of coal and other vital minerals.

Upper Silesia itself was destined to become one of the most important industrial districts in all of Europe with its vast production of coal, lead, zinc and iron, all of which were mined and utilised in factories on the spot.

Lower Silesia became almost purely Prussian.

It was left to the three Principalities in the centre to hold their heads high and maintain their independence.

All these thoughts passed through Zoleka's mind as she waited for her father to continue.

"We have succeeded in our country in proving our right to independence and I believe we have even gained the respect of our Prussian neighbours."

"You have been so wonderful, Papa, you know it is true. So diplomatic and tactful that they no longer despise us as they did at first."

He paused and Zoleka guessed what he was about to say.

"The exception," he went on, "is of course Krnov."

"You have said it before, Papa, but why is it so?"

"I feel the answer rests with Prince Majmir who has made no effort to be friendly with his free neighbours. In fact I know very little about him."

"But you have heard a great deal."

"What I have heard is not to his advantage. He is not bringing his country up to date as we have done here in Opava. He has not exploited his mineral resources as we have and I think, if he is not very careful, the Prussians will take his country over."

"They must not be allowed to do so," cried Zoleka. "If they did, they might think of invading us and Cieszyn."

"That is exactly what I thought myself," her father replied. "You are a clever girl and I might have known you would understand why I did not say 'no' immediately to the Prime Minister's suggestion."

"But what can I do? Even if I went as a Lady-in-Waiting, the Prince would hardly listen to me. I would just be miserable away from you and would not be of any use to Krnov."

"I just don't believe that's true. Because you are so intelligent, I do think you would be able to see for yourself

4

what is wrong at Krnov and make suggestions as to what could be done."

Zoleka did not answer.

He walked towards his desk and back again before he added,

"If I tried to interfere or even to pay a State visit to Krnov, they would undoubtedly tell me to mind my own business. What I do require is a great deal more inside information as to what is going on. If there is real danger, then I can consult with Cieszyn and together we must do everything we possibly can to ensure that we maintain our independence."

"I do understand what you are saying, Papa, but the whole idea is so frightening, and I do not wish to go away from *you*."

"Do you really think, my dearest, that I want to lose you? I love having you beside me and since you finished with governesses and tutors you have made me very happy. You have prevented me from feeling as miserable as I was when I first lost your mother."

"I know, Papa," Zoleka murmured gently. "And I still miss Mama more than I can ever say."

"How could either of us feel anything else?"

There was a note in his voice which spoke to her without words, the pain of losing her precious mother was just as acute as it had been when she died.

Hers had been such an unexpected death.

Princess Helen had seemed to be not only radiantly happy, but extremely healthy.

She paid many visits to the poor, which she firmly accepted as her duty.

Then while doing so, she had caught a foreign fever from a man who had just returned from the East.

The fever was unknown to all the local doctors who did not realise how serious it was.

By the time the Prince had urgently sent to Vienna for its most renowned physician, Princess Helen was dead.

It was a major blow to the whole Principality as she had been loved by everyone who knew her.

She was almost worshipped by the poor people in the City.

She had cared for them, assisted them and looked after them in a way that no ruling Princess of Opava had ever done in the country's history.

No less than her adoring husband and daughter, the people found it hard to believe that they had really lost her.

Princess Helen had been born English and a distant relative of Queen Victoria.

It had been an arranged Royal marriage and yet her husband had fallen head over heels in love with her straight from the moment they had first met.

She loved him in the same way as he loved her.

They were blissfully happy, although she regretted that she could not give her husband a son.

They absolutely adored their delightful and pretty daughter, who they both thought looked just like an angel sent to them from Heaven.

Thinking of her mother, Zoleka asked aloud,

"Do you think, Papa, that Mama would want me to go to Krnov?"

"I think your mother," her father answered quietly, "would feel that as we have received a cry for help, we are constrained to do something about it."

"A cry for help," Zoleka repeated almost beneath her breath. "Do you really think that is what it really is?"

"From what I have been told, the Prime Minister of Krnov and his Cabinet are feeling very worried. Reading between the lines I believe they are not as astute as they should be. But before I pass judgement I need a great deal more information."

"Which you think I would be able to find out for you?"

"You can but try, my dear. I am not only worried about Krnov, but about *us*."

Zoleka gave a little shudder.

The one thing no one ever wanted was to be under the yoke of the Prussians.

They were a most efficient people and there was no doubt at all that Upper Silesia had become richer since they had taken it over – but that was not to say that the Silesians were any happier under them.

There were frequent tales of persecution, besides a great number of protests against new and severe taxation.

There was a short poignant silence between father and daughter until Zoleka asked,

"If I do agree to go, Papa, how long must I stay?"

Prince Lászlé thought for a moment.

"Just long enough to find out everything we want to know. And whether you think that we should take a strong line before it is too late."

"That is the real question, Papa. If we are aware that things are in a bad way, you can be quite certain that the Prussians know it too."

"I am not too sure of that. According to the man I talked to this morning, the majority of the people of Krnov are content with their life as it is. It is the Prime Minister, who has not been in office for very long, who is worried that *laissez-faire* might prove disastrous to their country."

"As it has done in many places," remarked Zoleka.

She was very well read.

Not only was she very intelligent, but her father had a magnificent library.

He so enjoyed reading every new book which was published on any subject in which he was interested and Zoleka followed his example.

They enjoyed debating everything they had learned from each book, deliberately arguing just for the fun of it.

Secretly, because it was a mistake to make trouble unless it was absolutely necessary, they both disliked the Prussians.

They found it hard to convince themselves that the increase of prosperity both in Upper and Lower Silesia was worth the overweening presence of Prussians, who treated these countries contemptuously and their people like serfs.

At the same time they drew an enormous amount of advantage from them.

If there were failures the Prussians were very angry and more aggressive than usual.

When the gold and silver mines became exhausted, they squeezed what they could out of the peasants.

Each time this occurred the three free Principalities shivered and increased their defences.

But recently Krnov had not been following the lead of the other two.

They all realised that if it came to another war they would not be able to stand up against the vast resources of the Prussians.

There was no one alive who did not still yearn for the day when Silesia could look towards Vienna rather than the Prussian Hohenzollerns.

Zoleka walked towards the window.

The Palace garden was a mass of flowers and the white doves which her mother had introduced were flying round the fountain.

"How can I go away and leave you and this beauty which I love so much, Papa?"

"We could say 'no', tell them to go to hell and stay happy as we are. But we have to be honest and admit that may just be endangering our own people, the people your mother loved and who loved her, and who are, I think, still very happy."

"Of course they are so happy, Papa. You give them everything they have ever wanted. As you say, they loved Mama, and we also have a place in their hearts."

Her father sat down once more at his writing desk and then suddenly he brought his clenched fist down with a bang.

"Why on earth cannot Prince Majmir look after his people properly?" he demanded furiously. "It is now many years ago since he lost his wife and, I have heard, he was not particularly fond of her."

He paused before he continued bitterly,

"He has a daughter as I have you and he should be thinking of her rather than neglecting his country as he is so obviously doing at the moment."

"In what way, Papa?"

"His messenger was vague. He merely insinuated that the Prince was not at all interested in what goes on day by day. The country is left to the administration of the Krnov Cabinet and the last Prime Minister was apparently a disaster."

"So now the new one is attempting to modernise the government," remarked Zoleka.

"It is going to be a big task and of course I have not been told very much. It was just suggested by the Prime Minister that the Princess should have a Lady-in-Waiting capable of helping her take her place as the rightful heir to the throne."

Zoleka looked at her father in surprise.

"Prince Majmir is not thinking of abdicating?"

"I do hope not, but if he did, there would only be an ineffective and totally inexperienced young girl of eighteen to take his place."

"Which of course," Zoleka said almost beneath her breath, "would make an excellent excuse for the Prussians to walk in unopposed."

"You have said it for me, my bright daughter. That is exactly what I was thinking."

Zoleka gave a big sigh.

"I tell you what I will do, Papa. I will go to Krnov for a short time to see what is happening. Then I will insist on returning home to you, so that I can tell you what I have discovered."

She smiled as she added,

"Of course I could then have a serious illness which would prevent me from going back and they would have to find someone else in my place."

Her father held up his hands.

"You are going too fast," he protested. "One fence at a time. If you go, my dearest, you know it will break my heart to send you away. But I think you will be doing a great service not only in helping Krnov, but in making me and Prince Vaslov of Cieszyn aware of what is happening."

"What is Prince Vaslov like?"

"I have not seen him for some years – when he was finishing school and just about to go to University. When he left the latter, apparently with flying colours, he insisted on going round the world."

"That was sensible of him."

"When his father died six months ago, he took over as Ruler as everyone expected and I have been told that he is already bringing Cieszyn up-to-date in so many different ways."

"Well, that is certainly a step in the right direction at any rate. And if he has any brains he will support you in anything you suggest in the future."

"That is just what I need. We are three independent countries, but we have to be united. Otherwise we will be swallowed up by the Prussians as they have done in Upper and Lower Silesia and cease to be the individuals we are at the moment."

Zoleka gave a little sigh.

"Don't even think about it, Papa. It frightens me that those Prussians would so love to get their hands on our country and Krnov. Do not forget we both have mines and they are increasingly pleading for our lead, iron and zinc to supplement their own production."

"They are not going to have any of it, if I can help it and that is why, my precious little daughter, I want you to find out all you can about what is happening in Krnov."

He was silent for a moment before he added,

"I had actually set some enquiries in motion earlier. But when I heard nothing from Krnov and Prince Majmir never bothered to communicate with me, I thought it best to let sleeping dogs lie."

"I would have been only too glad to have agreed with you," sighed Zoleka.

"But now that they have approached me, it is very difficult to refuse. As I have already indicated, I feel that

11

someone with your fine intelligence could find out what is really happening."

"Do we have any diplomatic communication with Krnov?"

"There has been no reason for it. We want nothing from them and they apparently have wanted nothing from us until now."

The Prince rose and walked to the mantelpiece and then back again.

"I suppose if I am completely honest with myself, I have been worried for some time as to whether we should do something positive about Krnov. But there has been so much going on and it did not seem of great importance. So I ignored a little voice on my shoulder which told me that something was wrong."

"I will try to find out what it is, Papa."

Zoleka gave a deep sigh before she enquired,

"How soon do I have to go?"

"As soon as possible and let's get it over with, my dearest. I want you back here and it is going to be a very miserable month or so for me while you are away."

"Where is the envoy who came from Krnov to see you?"

"I sent him to talk to members of the Council. But I think they will get very little out of him. I sensed he was scared to say too much and had received strict instructions from his Prime Minister as to what he should and should not tell me."

"It does sound to me as if I am going to have a very hard time learning anything, Papa."

Her father smiled.

"And I have never known you not to learn what you wanted to learn. Also we must not forget that astute little

Third Eye of yours, which you used to talk about when you were a child."

When Zoleka was quite young, she had been given a book about Egypt.

In it she had seen that the Egyptian Pharaohs had a strange bump on their foreheads.

Her father explained to her at the time it was what the Egyptians called their 'Third Eye' and they used it to know the truth instinctively and clairvoyantly which other people failed to see.

Zoleka at the time had thought it amusing and she had walked about with a mark on her forehead, which she informed her father was her Third Eye.

He told her stories of how people had saved their lives by using their instinct and how others had made many precious discoveries. They had been made aware of many truths which were hidden from ordinary men and women.

Zoleka had practised using her intuition from the time she was twelve.

Now she sensed that she knew almost instantly the character and personality of men and women she met.

Long ago she had learnt that what she actually felt about them was in fact the truth.

At the time her father would encourage her to tell him exactly what she thought some dinner-guest was really like, and later he had her sitting with him when he engaged a new *aide-de-camp* or a servant.

"Now tell me what you think," he would say when the candidates left the room.

He was forced to admit that Zoleka was very clever in spotting a weakness in someone they had talked to.

As she grew older she used the same powers – to choose those whom she wished to be her friends.

She refused point blank to have one visitor at the Palace who was very anxious to be accepted, bringing her mother and Zoleka many bunches of flowers and presents and it was difficult not to accept the woman's kindness – and also not to invite her to any Royal festivities that were taking place.

"She is bad, Mama," Zoleka had said. "And I have no wish to accept her presents."

"You can hardly refuse them, dearest," her mother had said.

Zoleka had accepted the largesse and thanked the woman politely and then her mother found she had made a bonfire and burnt the presents until they were nothing but ashes.

"How could you do anything so foolish, Zoleka?" she asked. "If you did not want them yourself, there are plenty of girls your age who would be grateful for them."

"They are bad, Mama, and I do not want anyone to touch them," Zoleka insisted.

It was a year later that the woman in question was arrested for taking drugs.

She had violently resisted one of her staff who had tried to prevent her from taking more of them and the man was, in fact, so badly injured that he lost an arm and nearly died.

The woman was then barred from the Palace and was forced to leave the country.

Zoleka's father and mother were now compelled to admit that she had been right all along

"How did you know she was like that, dearest?" her mother enquired fervently.

Zoleka smiled.

"I looked at her with my Third Eye!"

When the young diplomat, Anton Bauer, who had travelled from Krnov to meet her father was introduced to Zoleka, she thought he was quite pleasant.

He was clearly frightened of saying the wrong thing concerning his visit.

Zoleka smiled at him.

"Do tell me about Princess Udele. Does she find it rather hard being an only child, as I have?"

"I expect so and it will be very nice for Her Royal Highness to have your company," replied Anton Bauer.

Zoleka asked him other questions about Krnov, all of which received rather vague answers.

She began to think like her father that perhaps the whole country was limp and ineffective.

In which case the Prussians would certainly start to infiltrate it.

As her father had said to her, the sooner she went to Krnov, the sooner it would all be over.

Zoleka agreed to the arrangements he had made and began to choose those whom she would take with her.

Marla, her lady's maid, was an obvious choice and she had been in her service for more than six years.

The *aide-de-camp* she next chose, Pieter Seitz, was a man of forty, whom she thought could visit places where she would be unable to go and he could talk to people she was unlikely to come into contact with

She was quite certain that he would be most useful in finding out what she needed to know.

*

Finally the day arrived when they were to travel to Krnov in two carriages.

It was not a particularly long journey, but some of the route was over mountainous roads.

The night before Zoleka left, she dined alone with her father, which they always enjoyed so much more than when they had to have other people with them.

"You must take extra good care of yourself, Papa, whilst I am away and think of me every day."

"You know I will be doing so and I shall miss our rides and the times like this when we can be together and talk without being afraid of being overheard."

"That is one problem I was thinking about. Do you imagine that the Palace in Krnov has concealed holes in the walls through which a spy can see or overhear? We have been told so often of how this can happen in Russia and in many other countries."

"I think you will find, my dearest Zoleka, that they will treat you just as a charming young girl, who will be a nice companion for the young Princess."

He smiled before he continued,

"I don't think that Anton Bauer would believe for a single moment that you might be an Ambassador for your country."

"An Ambassador with a keen eye and ear who will miss nothing!" exclaimed Zoleka.

"What you must not do is to put anything down in writing," her father warned.

"Then how am I to tell you what I have found out?"

"I think the wisest way would be to take a second *aide-de-camp* with you who we trust. He can always be sent backwards and forwards ostensibly with gifts and to fetch items for you, but really to tell me what you want me to know."

Zoleka clasped her hands together.

"You are quite right, Papa, we should have thought of it before. If it is something very serious I will come back myself, but if we take a special messenger, he will make me feel I can reach you very quickly if I want to."

"You are not to anticipate anything really nasty or untoward happening. If you do, it might perhaps prejudice you unreasonably."

"It would not do that, Papa, it is just that I think we should be prepared."

"I am afraid you may be disappointed, my dearest. You will find Krnov exceedingly dull and may learn very little after all."

Zoleka threw up her hands.

"Now you are trying to put me off the trip, Papa! You know I will find it dreadfully boring. In which case I will return home at once and then the Krnovians will have to look after themselves."

"I have the feeling that is what Prince Majmir really wants. It is only that I am so very frightened of losing our independence, which is so precious to us all."

"Of course it is, Papa, and something we must not lose whatever happens. I will do my best and no one can do more."

"I wouldn't mind betting that your best will be very good indeed, as it always has been."

"Now you are flattering me and I love it!"

"When you come back," her father suggested, "we will throw a ball, which will be the finest ball we have ever given."

He put his hand over hers.

"I am feeling rather guilty that I have not given you enough parties, which your mother would have wanted for you now that you are eighteen."

"I have been perfectly happy riding with you, Papa, and doing all the things we have done. The balls can wait and so can all the young men, who I do know at the back of your mind you believe should be around to amuse me."

Her father smiled at her.

"I admit I have been rather selfish. I have wanted you all to myself and have not concentrated on counting up how many eligible young gentlemen there are to be found in the neighbourhood!"

"If you mean eligible for me to marry, Papa, I can tell you here and now that I do not wish to marry anyone – for several years at least!"

"Why do you say that?"

"Because it would be so terrible to be forced into an unhappy arranged marriage. You and dear Mama were so happy, but of course it was a million to one chance against that you should have fallen in love with each other. You could so easily have hated each other and then what would have happened?"

"If I am honest, that was what I was afraid of, but it was so very important for our country that I should have a Consort, and no one could have been more fortunate for us all than your darling mother."

"That is why I am now asking how I can be sure of being equally lucky."

"We will just have to pray that Heaven is listening to our plea and you must now use your Third Eye on every unfortunate individual who lays his heart at your feet!"

Zoleka laughed.

"I am not going to worry at all about the ones who lay their hearts at my feet. It is those who will say I would be of great assistance in building up their own country or keeping the enemies from the gate who frighten me!"

Prince Lászlé knew exactly what she was saying.

He realised that because of her rank it was exactly what might happen to her in the future.

"Forget it, Zoleka," he told her affectionately. "Just believe you will find real happiness as I did and it will be when you least expect it."

"That is so exactly what I want to believe. When I marry I want to be as happy as Mama was with you – "

"And as I was with your mother," her father ended.

She realised by the sad expression in his eyes that once again he was grieving over the wife he had lost. He was obviously feeling that nothing could ever be the same without her.

Zoleka rose and placed her arms round her father's neck.

"What we have both have to believe, Papa, is that Mama is guiding us and maybe it is Mama herself who has suggested to the Krnov Prime Minister that he should do something urgently about his country."

"It is what I would like to believe, Zoleka, and then I should not feel so guilty in sending you there, because I know instinctively it is going to be very dull for you."

"I shall have to think of some way of livening it up, Papa! In the meantime concentrate on thinking how soon I can come back to you."

"I will certainly do so," he promised her, "and you must be quick in finding out all I want to know."

Zoleka gave a little sigh.

"I can only hope the Palace is busy like ours – with people coming in and out and something happening every half-hour! And you and I knowing that the people in the City around us are all happy and contented."

Her father laughed, but he did not comment.

Then Zoleka continued,

"Instead of which I have a feeling that their Palace will be filled with a fleet of courtiers bowing and curtsying every few minutes. The food will be horrible and nothing will happen unless there is a thunder-storm from one week to the next!"

The Prince chuckled as she meant him to do.

"It could not possibly be as bad as that!"

"Mama warned me that that was what most Palaces, where she had stayed, were like. She had found them so dull, which made her so determined that here in our Palace life would always be fun with everybody laughing."

"That is exactly what your mother achieved and I think you and I have carried it on."

"Of course we have, Papa. But if you expect me to create that wonderful atmosphere out of nothing in Krnov, you are mistaken."

"Now do not be prejudiced before you actually get there," he warned her. "Then if you have to wake them up with a bang – do so and come back to me quickly."

"That is exactly what I am planning to do!"

She put her arms round her father's neck again and kissed him.

"The trouble is, Papa, there are not enough Princes like you in the world to make it as much fun as it should be."

Her father did not say any more, but kissed her on her cheek.

Only when Zoleka retired to bed did she think her father would undoubtedly be lonely and miserable without her.

'I think my real duty is here with Papa,' she mused, 'rather than trying to cheer up some obscure and tiresome people who have not the sense to amuse themselves.'

As she undressed, she recalled the real reason why she was being sent to Krnov.

The Prussians with their gaudy uniforms, their guns and long marching columns of men were waiting poised on the borders.

One day they would march straight into the country and Krnov would lose its independence overnight.

'I have to save them from that ghastly nightmare, if I possibly can,' she determined.

At the same time she had not the slightest idea how she could possibly do it.

She did not want her father to find out, but she was feeling afraid.

CHAPTER TWO

Before Anton Bauer started out for Krnov to report that Her Royal Highness, Princess Zoleka, would be most delighted to be Lady-in-Waiting to Princess Udele, Zoleka had a long talk with him.

Her father was back working on his book, so there was no interruption.

She was quite determined to find out as much as she could about the Palace in Krnov.

"Tell me all about it," she urged him coaxingly.

He seemed more relaxed than he had been with her father.

"As a matter of fact, Your Royal Highness, I have brought with me a plan of the Palace, thinking I might be asked for it."

"That was most thoughtful of you," she remarked to him flatteringly. "Please let me see it."

He had it with him and took it out of his pocket and he showed her the entrance which seemed impressive and the reception rooms on the ground floor.

There was a staircase going up to the next floor.

"Is that where the State rooms are?" she asked.

Anton nodded.

"That is right, Your Royal Highness, although I am afraid they are usually empty as we do not entertain very often these days."

"That must be very boring for the Princess now she is eighteen," replied Zoleka.

There was no answer to her remark from Anton, so she next looked carefully at the plan of the State rooms.

"You have quite a number of them. Tell me which is the prettiest."

"They are all named after flowers," Anton replied, "and everyone admires the one which is called 'Roses'."

"I suppose it is decorated in pink!"

She looked at the wings of the Palace and asked,

"Now where does Her Royal Highness sleep?"

"The schoolroom and the Princess's bedroom are located on the second floor of the East Wing,"

"And she has not moved out now she is grown up?"

"Oh, no!"

Zoleka said no more about the Palace, but enquired about her arrival.

"Your Royal Highness will be greeted at the border of our two countries," Anton told her, "and as I have had the privilege of meeting you, I expect I shall be sent with a carriage to convey you to the Palace."

He thought that Princess Zoleka was looking a little disappointed as if she expected a more formal welcome.

He added quickly,

"There is a good Posting inn just inside the border and I thought you would like to stop there for luncheon."

"That is a good idea," agreed Zoleka. "I expect you have already been told that I shall have an *aide-de-camp* with me as well as my lady's maid who will travel with the luggage."

"I will make all the necessary arrangements, Your Royal Highness," he promised.

When he had left, Zoleka thought over what he had told her.

She decided that she must, as her father had urged, wake up the Palace at Krnov with a bang.

She did not, however, say anything to her father but made plans in her own mind.

To her lady's maid, Marla, she said,

"I have to appear impressive and there is no time to purchase any more clothes. What is there in my wardrobe that will make the Krnovians look up, if nothing else?"

There was a pause before Marla replied tentatively,

"Your Royal Highness knows that your mother's beautiful gowns will fit you."

"Of course they will and I know Mama would not mind my using them when I have a very important reason for doing so."

She and Marla walked into her mother's room.

It had been left exactly as it was after she had died and her father had ordered that nothing was to be moved.

Zoleka knew he often went to her room by himself, feeling that he was with his beloved wife again.

All the gowns that her mother had bought for State occasions were hanging in the wardrobe and they had been carefully looked after by the Palace housekeeper.

She chose three that glittered with diamante, which had been worn by her mother on special occasions like the Opening of Parliament or a wedding of a relative.

There was one gown her mother had worn at a huge ball that had been given at the Palace.

Zoleka had been too young to attend it, but she had, however, been allowed to watch all the glamorous dancers from the balcony.

She could remember how beautiful her mother had looked as she received the guests and opened the ball with her father.

Zoleka now went to the wardrobe-room next door, where there were hats, wraps to wear in the evening and a great many attractive handbags.

She and Marla chose what they thought was most suitable for her – and they were all far grander than any she would ever have worn at home.

Again Zoleka did not tell her father, as she thought it might upset him, although he had, in fact, suggested she should take some of her mother's jewellery with her.

"Now you are older you can wear pearls round your neck," he conceded, "and very occasionally bracelets in the evening."

He smiled lovingly at her before adding,

"You are so lovely, my dearest girl, that you do not really need gems to make you glitter."

Zoleka kissed him for the compliment.

She packed the jewels most carefully into a case as she knew the loss of any of them would upset her father – they were such a strong link with the wife he had adored.

For her arrival at the Krnov Palace, she put on one of her mother's smartest dresses.

But she did not wear a hat when she went down to breakfast with her father.

She thought he would not remember the gown, but undoubtedly he would notice the hat was a lot smarter than anything she had worn when she went out with him to visit someone in the City or attend a banquet.

However he was not concerned at that moment with her looks, but that he was losing her.

"I shall miss you every moment you are away, my

dearest," he admitted. "And it would be quite safe for you to write to me, if it is only to tell me you are missing me."

"You know I shall be doing just that, Papa. I will send Pieter Seitz back with any information which I think is especially significant."

"I think you are wise to have chosen him. He is an intelligent man and I have told him I want to know what is concerning the ordinary citizens of Krnov with whom you would not be able to circulate."

"I have chosen as my other *aide-de-camp* someone who can come backwards and forwards more often. And it is someone who may surprise you."

"Who is it?"

"Count von Hofmannstall."

Her father looked at Zoleka in astonishment.

"The Count! Why on earth have you invited him?"

"For one reason because I want to impress or rather wake up the Prince and his entourage at the Palace. Also because the Count is such an intelligent young gentleman and will perhaps be able to find out more about His Royal Highness than I am able to do."

Prince László remained silent as he was thinking.

Franz von Hofmannstall was the youngest member of one of the most distinguished and influential families in Austria.

His father, the Arch-Duke, son of the Emperor of Austria, was well known and welcome in many countries in Europe.

He had sent his son to Opava because the Prince's horses were so famous and young Franz was very anxious to become an even better rider than he was already.

The Arch-Duke, who was a long-standing friend of Prince László, had written,

"It will be very good for Franz to have a change of air, but I don't wish him at the moment to go too far away.

I am therefore sending him to you where I know he will be very thrilled with your horses and learn to ride as brilliantly as you do yourself.

It is also most important for him to get to know all about the three Austrian Principalities that are still free of the Prussian yoke.

But to mix with people it is wiser for him not to use his real title. He will therefore just be the Count Franz von Hofmannstall."

Prince Lászlé had welcomed Count Franz to Opava with open arms, but he was just a little perturbed that his daughter was now taking him away with her.

"I will not keep him long, Papa," Zoleka said as she read his thoughts, "but it will be very good for him to see what Krnov is really like and it is he who will be bringing you the most secret reports I will be sending you."

"I see your reasoning, my dearest, and of course it is most intelligent of you."

"Thank you, Papa. I have asked the Count to ride in charge of my Mounted Escort."

She paused for a moment before she added,

"I have also asked him to choose the six men who will form the Escort."

The Prince threw back his head and laughed.

"You are certainly doing it in style, dearest, but you are quite right! Let them see from the very beginning that you intend to behave as Royalty which, from what I hear, they are not doing in Krnov."

They did not hurry over breakfast because the border was only three hours drive away and if they were to arrive at luncheon time, there was no reason to leave before ten o'clock.

Zoleka made the most of the time with her father.

Only when it was nearly ten did she go upstairs to put on her hat and make sure Marla had packed everything they required.

When she came down again the two carriages were outside the door.

The one Zoleka was to travel in was large and most imposing. It was the one her father always used on State occasions and was drawn by four perfectly matched white stallions.

The coachman and footman were dressed in Opava State livery and looked extremely smart.

Zoleta had already told the Count that they were to arrive with a flourish and all flags flying!

He too was dressed in his smartest uniform with a splendid feathered hat and he was riding one of her father's most spiritcd and best-bred horses.

The Escort consisted of six uniformed Cavalrymen who were also beautifully turned out.

There was a distinct smile and a twinkle in the eyes of Prince Lászlé when he saw his daughter off.

"Goodbye, darling Papa," she called. "I am trying to think of this as the beginning of an adventure, but I keep wishing you were coming with me."

"I would find it very amusing. You must write and tell me all about their reactions to your appearance. It will undoubtedly be a shock to the Krnovians!"

"That is just what I intend it to be!"

She put her arms round her father's neck.

"Please, darling Papa, think of me and pray for me. Without you it is all rather frightening."

"You can be sure I shall be praying for you every day and missing you."

He kissed her again as she stepped into the carriage.

Pieter Seitz, also smartly dressed, was in attendance and they drove off.

Zoleka waved to her father until they were out of sight.

She could see with some satisfaction that they were being followed by another large carriage in which Marla was sitting with all the luggage.

*

The horses were fresh and they moved swiftly over the roads which the Prince had insisted must be improved all over Opava.

"If there is one thing I dislike," he had often said, "it is rough rocky roads when they need not be so."

He had therefore given a great deal of employment to men out of work and they had widened and resurfaced the roads in every part of the Principality.

As they drove along, Zoleka said to Pieter Seitz,

"I know my Papa has told you why we are going and how important our mission is, but maybe we are being over-anxious. We may find that Krnov is much more up-to-date than we expect and all our fears are groundless."

"That is the news I hope to take back to His Royal Highness," replied Pieter. "But from what I gathered from the envoy who brought us the Prime Minister's request and who I understand will be meeting us at the border, things are even worse than we have heard already."

"I thought maybe you would get him to talk, Pieter. He was too frightened of Papa to give him the information he wanted and he thought I was far too young and frivolous to be interested in anything serious."

Pieter laughed.

"It is because Your Royal Highness is so pretty few people realise what a clever brain you have."

"Well, we do not want them to be aware of that too quickly in Krnov. If they do believe I am just a superficial young woman, they will not be guarding their tongues. We want to know the worst as speedily as possible."

"That is what His Royal Highness has said, but I am afraid it may take longer than he hopes."

"We can only do our very best and I would like to tell you how very pleased I am, Pieter, to have you with me and to be able to rely on you."

"I promise I will not fail Your Royal Highness."

They drove on and as they approached the border, the country became a little wilder.

Not far away was a range of low mountains where many minerals were mined that contributed so much to the great prosperity of Opava.

The same range extended into Krnov and as far as Zolcka had been able to ascertain, nothing was being done about them on their side of the border.

The Krnovians had not employed, as her father had done, experts from all over Europe to find what minerals the mountains actually contained.

'How can they be so incredibly stupid?' she asked herself now, seeing the mountains stretch out into the far distance, the sunshine dazzling on their peaks.

As they crossed the border she saw that this part of Krnov was very like her own country, but it seemed to be almost uninhabited. The people they did see were poorly dressed and their cottages were in a bad state of repair.

As Anton Bauer had said, the inn where they were to have luncheon was just a short distance from the border.

They drew up outside it at exactly one o'clock and Anton was there to meet them.

He stared in a mixture of amazement and surprise at

the Princess's Escort with the Count riding ahead of her carriage.

As Zoleka stepped out, he bowed and greeted her to the State of Krnov.

"Are you alone?" she asked in an astonished voice.

"I was asked to meet Your Royal Highness," Anton replied, "because we had met before, but I did not know that Your Royal Highness would be expecting a Mounted Escort."

Zoleka gave a little cry.

"But, of course, I always have one! Papa would not think of letting me drive about without one."

As Anton looked somewhat crestfallen, she said,

"Never mind. My Escort, which is commanded by Count von Hoffmannstall, will, of course, take me to your Palace."

As they were talking they were moving towards the door of the inn.

Zoleka could see in the courtyard that there was a carriage drawn by only two horses.

She stopped and exclaimed,

"I have an idea! As they will not be expecting me to arrive so quickly as I would with four horses, I think it would be wise if you went back now to inform the Prime Minister, the Lord Chamberlain, and of course Her Royal Highness Princess Udele, that I will be arriving sooner than they expect."

She continued in a more considerate tone of voice,

"I am sure that they would be very upset if I arrived before they were ready to receive me."

She recognised as she spoke from the expression on Anton's face that the Prime Minister had not considered it necessary to receive her and the same probably applied to the Lord Chamberlain.

Before Anton could reply, she added,

"And you must, of course, tell these gentlemen that I have also brought Count von Hoffmannstall with me as my second *aide-de-camp* besides Pieter Seitz whom I think you met when you were staying with us."

She paused a moment.

"The Count is the youngest son of one of the most important grandees at the Palace in Vienna and I feel sure that His Royal Highness Prince Majmir will be delighted to meet him."

By this time they had stepped into the inn where the proprietor was bowing almost to the ground.

"Luncheon be ready for Your Royal Highness," he said. "And I hope very much it'll be to your liking."

"I am sure it will be. We will be three for luncheon and will you see to it that there is a meal for my Escort and for my lady's maid who is in the carriage just behind us."

"It'll be seen to, Your Royal Highness," agreed the proprietor bowing even lower than before.

They went into luncheon.

Zoleka found that it was an adequate but dull meal.

Champagne had not been ordered for them.

Her father would always arrange for champagne to be served whenever he greeted anyone of significance on the borders of Opava.

Anton now held a whispered conversation with the proprietor.

Zoleka guessed it was to reassure him that he would be paid for the additional guests, but that he did not have enough money with him.

'No one,' she pondered with a glint of satisfaction, 'at the Krnov Palace will have expected me to arrive with such a retinue.'

She was only hoping they would be as astonished as Anton was.

As she sat down to luncheon with her two *aides-de-camp*, she knew they were as amused at the situation as she was herself.

"Poor young Bauer will be hungry," smiled Pieter, "as you sent him off without his luncheon."

"Can you imagine my Papa treating any guest when they arrived in Opava in the way we have been? It is not Anton's fault of course, but it is the Prime Minister who should know better."

"I heard they had all become lazy and neglectful of protocol in Krnov," remarked Pieter. "But I think you can be sure now they will be on the doorstep when Your Royal Highness arrives!"

The Count too thought that this was a good joke.

He told Zoleka stories of how he and his father had been received in different countries.

"When I was travelling for several months after I left University," he recounted, "things were very different. I did not use my title as I wanted to see how the ordinary people behaved and I think it was a good experience."

"Of course it was," agreed Zoleka, "and I admire you very much for doing it. You will find it a great help in the future if you are going into the Diplomatic Service."

"That is what I may do," the Count replied, "but my father has such extensive possessions all over Austria that at present, as he is not in such good health, I find myself running from one to the other to make sure everything is in order as he would wish it to be."

He spoke in a manner that told Zoleka he enjoyed being in control and having people obeying him.

She thought, as she had before, that he would be of great assistance to her and also that what they were going to experience shortly in Krnov would be of considerable help to him in the future.

They did not hurry over their luncheon.

When eventually they drove off again the sun was shining.

The part of the country they were now entering was more attractive than the borderland, but here too, however, the people looked poor and badly dressed.

The houses were not well built and a great number of them were in need of repair and they passed through several small towns that did not seem at all prosperous.

Once again Zoleka was thinking how stupid it was of Prince Majmir not to develop coal and other minerals in his country as her father and Prince Vaslov were doing.

*

It took them under two hours to reach the Capital of Krnov where the Palace was situated.

The Capital certainly looked more prosperous and the houses were much better built, but the citizens looked apathetic.

They stared in amazement at the Princess's carriage and her Escort and yet there was no question of cheering or waving as her own people always did to her and her father.

The Palace, as they approached it, seemed to look impressive. It was high above the City and being built of white stone was at least conspicuous.

Zolita's Mounted Escort looked very smart as they turned in through the gates.

The sentries came immediately to attention.

There was a long driveway passing through gardens bright with blossom, but they did not compare in any way, Zoleka thought, with the gardens at home.

She had tidied herself at the inn before she left and now she took a quick glance at her face in the little mirror in her handbag.

With her eyes shining and the sun catching the glint in her fair hair, she looked very lovely in her mother's hat.

The carriage came slowly to a standstill outside the large doors of the Palace.

Zoleka saw Anton Bauer waiting for her and behind him, just in the doorway, were three people.

"He has done it," she whispered to Pieter. "I am sure that is the Prime Minister and the Lord Chamberlain."

"Your Royal Highness was very clever to get them here," replied Pieter.

The carriage door was now opened by a footman in Royal Livery.

Zoleka stepped out.

She walked towards the one female in the reception party who she guessed must be Princess Udele.

She realised as she did so that the Princess was very pretty, but looking rather frightened.

In fact she saw the Lord Chamberlain put his hand on her back as if to push her forward.

Zoleka kissed her on both cheeks.

"It is delightful to meet Your Royal Highness," she said, "after so many years of being kept apart."

"Welcome to Krnov," greeted Princess Udele in a faltering voice. "We are very honoured to have you here."

It was obviously what she had been told to say.

Zoleka replied,

"And I am so pleased to be here in Krnov. It will be very exciting, I hope, for both of us."

She then turned to the Prime Minister and held out her hand. He bowed over it and made a long speech of welcome, which he had quite obviously made many times before.

Then Zoleka turned to the Lord Chamberlain.

He welcomed her briefly before asking in what she thought was rather a sharp voice,

"I can see Your Royal Highess has brought a large Escort with you. Will they be riding back tonight?"

Zoleka gave a cry of horror.

"Oh, no! It would be far too much for the horses. I hope you will be kind enough to permit them to stay for the night. And may I first present to Her Royal Highness and of course to you, Count Franz von Hoffmannstall who has graciously come with me as my *aide-de-camp*."

She glanced at the Prime Minister before adding,

"I expect you have met some of his distinguished family in Vienna. Count Franz is a brilliant horseman and we are delighted he has come to stay with us in Opava."

The Prime Minister and the Lord Chamberlain were all bows and politeness.

There were no Austrians who were not aware of the Hofmannstalls and the part they had played in the history of Austria.

They moved inside the Palace.

The hall, thought Zoleka, was fairly imposing but shabby.

"Would Your Royal Highness like to retire to your room before we have tea which I have arranged for you in the Blue drawing room?" the Lord Chamberlain asked.

"I have been thinking about my room on the way here," responded Zoleka. "When I saw a plan of the Palace

I was very impressed. I do so hope that I shall be given the State room which I am told is the prettiest."

A startled expression came into the eyes of the Lord Chamberlain.

She knew he had never for a moment contemplated her residing in one of the State rooms.

"I am sure you will know the room I am referring to," continued Zoleka. "It is the Rose room and as the rose is my favourite flower I shall be very disappointed if I have been allocated any other room."

There was nothing the Lord Chamberlain could do.

He muttered that he would, of course, escort her to the Rose room if that was what she wanted.

Zoleka smiled at Princess Udele.

"I do not know where Her Royal Highness might be sleeping, but of course it will be so much more convenient, as we have so much to do together, if we are close to one another. I saw on the plan of the Palace that the boudoir of the Rose room adjoins the Lily room. I am sure that would be a very appropriate room for Her Royal Highness."

Before the Lord Chamberlain could protest Princess Udele piped up,

"I have been made to continue sleeping next to the schoolroom even though my governess has left. I would love to be in the Lily room – it is *very* pretty."

"Then it shall be arranged," the Lord Chamberlain conceded rather reluctantly.

It was obvious from the way he spoke that he was not only surprised but very annoyed, but for the moment he could not think how he could refuse to do what was asked without being extremely rude.

"That will be wonderful," enthused Zoleka. "We shall be able to chatter about things and have a comfortable

37

place to relax when we are not busy entertaining people in the reception rooms."

Again she noted a startled expression on the Lord Chamberlain's face.

It was then that the Prime Minister asked,

"Is Your Royal Highness hoping to entertain many guests whilst you are here?"

"Of course I am. I understood I was to come here to help Princess Udele in taking up her Royal duties having finished with her education."

"But of course," the Prime Minister agreed. "Your Royal Highness is quite right."

"I would very much like to talk to you about the arrangements for tomorrow, so please arrange a meeting."

Before the Prime Minister could respond to Zoleka, she had turned to the Lord Chamberlain.

"I do wish to wash and take off my hat after such a long journey. Will you be kind enough please to show me the way to the Rose room."

She walked to the staircase as she spoke and started to climb up it.

The Lord Chamberlain followed her.

At the top of the stairs, Zoleka found, as indeed she had expected, the housekeeper was waiting for her. There was no mistaking her in a rustling black dress and a huge silver chatelaine at her waist.

"This is Frau Leuger, the Palace housekeeper, who will be looking after Your Royal Highness," said the Lord Chamberlain.

She bobbed a curtsy and Zoleka held out her hand.

"It is so very nice for me to be here in Krnov, and I am looking forward to seeing the Rose room, which I have heard is so beautiful."

She saw the housekeeper look with astonishment at the Lord Chamberlain, who instructed her quickly,

"Her Royal Highness will be sleeping in the Rose room and Princess Udele will be in the Lily room."

"This is something I was not expecting, my Lord," the housekeeper replied, "but of course both the rooms are unoccupied."

The Lord Chamberlain did not deign to answer and the housekeeper led the way along the corridor.

The State rooms were certainly magnificent, but it was very obvious that they had not been in use for a long time.

There was the smell of a room where the windows had not regularly been opened and although they were not dusty, there were no flowers on the tables.

The curtains were drawn tight until the housekeeper pulled them back.

"This is quite delightful!" exclaimed Zoleka. "And I would like my maid to be brought up to me as quickly as possible so that she can help me with my hair after I have removed my hat."

The Lord Chamberlain walked out into the passage and the housekeeper followed him.

To her amusement Zoleka could hear them arguing with each other about the rooms.

Princess Udele had also come upstairs, but no one had paid much attention to her.

Now she said to Zoleka,

"It is very kind of you to suggest that I should come downstairs. When I asked before, they said I was to stay in the same room that I have always used, which is next to the schoolroom and not very pretty."

Zoleka smiled at her.

"That room must now be closed up and forgotten. You are grown-up and important, otherwise they would not have asked me to come and be with you. We are going to have a lot of fun, even if some of the old fuddy-duddies in the Palace will be surprised at what we will do!"

Udele clasped her hands together.

"Do you think we can have a party?"

"Of course we can have a party. We can have lots of parties. But first of all we must find out who the young people in your country are and where we can find them."

"I have never been allowed to meet any of them," she answered. "Papa is not interested in me and I have just been left with my governess."

Zoleka smiled at her.

"That is all in the past and now you and I are going to have fun. But you will have to support me in everything we want to do."

"Of course I will. Thank you so much for coming, Princess Zoleka, it is very kind of you."

Zoleka removed her hat and was wondering what had happened to Marla when she arrived.

"You would not believe it, Your Royal Highness," she spluttered, as she came into the room. "We was taken up the stairs and you've never seen such an uncomfortable little room they was giving to you. And not a place to hang your gowns!"

"I thought that might happen," laughed Zoleka.

She turned to Udele.

"This is Marla, my precious maid. She has looked after me for six years and I am sure she will give your maid lots of tips as to how to make you even prettier than you are already."

"I do not have a maid all to myself."

"But you must have your own maid! I shall explain that you will need one to look after your new clothes."

"New clothes, Princess Zoleka?"

"I expect you to tell me which are the best and most exclusive shops in this City, because you will have to buy new clothes for all the activities we are going to do. I am absolutely certain that no one has ever thought about you acquiring the clothes that every *debutante* is entitled to."

Udele gave a skip of joy.

"I would so love some new clothes," she enthused. "Those I have were made by the Palace seamstress and she always makes everything in just the same patterns she has used for years. I just hate all my dresses, but when I have complained no one listens to me."

"*I* will listen to you, Udele, but now we must hurry and go down to tea. Marla will see to everything here."

"You can leave it all to me, Your Royal Highness," Marla now piped up. "I knew you wouldn't put up with that nonsense of being pushed away in what had once been the nurseries!"

She spoke with such contempt that Zoleka giggled.

Then slipping her arm through Udele's, she urged,

"Now come along. We have such a lot to do and so much to plan. You must help me jump the hedges which stand in our way as quickly as possible."

The two girls were laughing as they ran down the stairs.

The large reception room where they were having tea was fairly comfortable, but Zoleka considered that it lacked a woman's touch.

There were no flowers, which she knew would have displeased her mother.

The Lord Chamberlain and the Prime Minister were waiting for them.

"I thought that Your Royal Highness would wish to pour out the tea," suggested the Lord Chamberlain rather severely.

"But, of course, and I am quite sure that your Chef has prepared some delicious cakes and scones for us to eat after rather a dull luncheon."

There was a pause and somewhat uncomfortably the Lord Chamberlain responded,

"I am afraid that I did not think of sending any food from the Palace with Anton Bauer, when he went to meet you."

"It is just what my father would always do," replied Zoleka. "And of course some champagne too, which most people find refreshing after a long journey."

"I can only promise that you will have it tonight," the Lord Chamberlain muttered.

Zoleka smiled at him and then asked,

"May I have an audience with His Royal Highness now or shall I wait until dinner?"

There was a silence after she had spoken.

She realised, as indeed she had expected, that it had never crossed the Lord Chamberlain's mind that she would have dinner with Prince Majmir.

After another uncomfortable moment had passed he said,

"Usually Princess Udele has supper alone."

"Supper!" exclaimed Zoleka. "But surely now that she has grown up and is old enough to take on a Lady-in-Waiting, she must naturally have dinner with her father and any guests staying at the Palace."

She paused before she continued,

"I should be glad to arrange some dinner parties as

soon as you help me with the names of the available young people and we would enjoy dancing afterwards."

If she had dropped a bomb, the Lord Chamberlain could not have been more astonished.

Before he could speak, Zoleka carried on,

"I can see you are surprised. But you must realise that now Princess Udele has grown up she must take her place and play her part as heiress to the throne as she has not yet done."

The Lord Chamberlain still could not speak.

"The first step forward is for Her Royal Highness to meet young people of her own age. Then I am sure that the Prime Minister will arrange a number of important public engagements for her."

She smiled confidently at Udele, who spoke up as if she had been prompted,

"It all sounds so exciting. It has been so dull these last months, staying upstairs with nothing to do when I was not taken out riding."

"For the future," asserted Zoleka, "it will not be a question of people taking you out. You will be giving your orders as to where and when you want to go, and as I love riding we will ride as much as we can and on your father's best horses."

She paused for a moment before she added,

"You will find that Count Franz von Hofmannstall is such an outstanding rider. He will be only too willing to accompany us."

As if the Lord Chamberlain felt the conversation was going too far, he addressed Udele,

"I feel sure Your Royal Highness will understand we must have approval of all this from your father. I do not think he realised, when the Prime Minister asked that you

43

should have a Lady-in-Waiting, that so much change would be involved with the appointment."

"Of course, if you do not want me here," interposed Zoleka, "I easily can go home. I can assure you I have left a great many duties behind me and my father is missing me very much."

"There is no question of that," the Prime Minister intervened. "We are very delighted to have you here and I think it is so important that, as you suggest, Princess Udele should meet the people in the country, who have not even seen her before, let alone met her."

"That is certainly something we can put right, and as I have already said to Princess Udele, the first thing we are going to do is to go shopping."

"Shopping!" cried out the Lord Chamberlain. "But why?"

"Because every *debutante* is entitled to a trousseau. I have a suspicion, and I am sure I am right, that the poor Princess is still wearing the same clothes she wore in the schoolroom. But now she is eighteen and is 'coming out'."

"Of course you are right," the Prime Minister came in. "And I can see by the way Your Royal Highness is dressed that you would know exactly the sort of clothes our Princess should be wearing."

"And what I want to wear," added Princess Udele. "It will be very very wonderful to have new clothes."

"You shall have the very best that can be provided here," insisted Zoleka, "and if they are not good enough, we will send off to Vienna. I brought some lovely gowns from Vienna only last year."

If she had not been concentrating on playing her part, she could not have helped laughing at the expression on the Lord Chamberlain's face.

It had never struck him for a single minute that this sort of situation would arise from the Princess taking on a Lady-in-Waiting.

He had supposed she would be some mousey little woman who would feel very honoured to be in the Palace – someone who would just carry out her duties obediently without having an idea or thought of her own.

Zoleka poured out another cup of tea for the Prime Minister and she was aware that he was quietly amused by the Lord Chamberlain's consternation.

Almost as if he had been prompted, the latter rose to his feet.

"I think if Your Royal Highness will excuse me," he said to Zoleka, "I will go and see His Royal Highness and inform him of your arrival."

"Tell him I am anxious to make his acquaintance. I quite understand that he was too busy to greet us when we arrived, but I feel that when he has the time we will have a great deal to discuss."

The Lord Chamberlain left the room.

The Prime Minister looked at Zoleka and sighed,

"Might I congratulate Your Royal Highness? You have started to blow away the cobwebs even quicker than I hoped. In fact, I can only thank you from the bottom of my heart for coming to Krnov."

"Thank you, but I shall need your help."

"You have only to ask," he answered, "and I will support you in every way I can."

Before Zoleka could say any more the door opened and the Count and Pieter Seitz entered.

"We were told Your Royal Highness was in here," Pieter said to Zoleka, "and I have come to assure you that the horses are all comfortably bedded down and their riders are now looking forward to finding out what are the gayest places to visit in the City."

"Then you have done your work splendidly. Let me pour you a cup of tea."

Both men accepted and the Prime Minister said to the Count,

"Tell me how your father is. I am a great admirer of his and perhaps one day I can persuade him to pay us a visit here in Krnov."

"If you were to invite him, I think he would enjoy it. In the meantime I would like to meet as many of your citizens as I possibly can. I always enjoy meeting people and visiting a new country where I have not been before."

"That is a tall order," responded the Prime Minister, "but I will do my very best to fulfil it. There are a number of people I think would interest you. But please remember I myself have only just recently been appointed, so I have to tread very carefully."

"To miss the old people's corns," smiled the Count. "They are always getting in the way of new ideas and new interests. We too have had exactly the same trouble on my father's estate, but I have managed to introduce quite a lot of new methods."

"Then I congratulate you. The most difficult thing in the world is to pour new wine into an old bottle!"

They all laughed at this remark and then the Count asked Zoleta,

"What is the programme, Your Royal Highness, for tonight?"

"That is just what I am waiting to hear. Apparently Princess Udele has not yet been allowed to come down to dinner. Now I have demanded that she should, there is a revolution going on among those who sit at the top table!"

Everyone smiled.

And then the Count seated himself beside Udele.

"And what do you think about it all, Your Royal Highness?" he asked.

"I think it is the most wonderful thing that has ever happened here. You have arrived as if you had dropped down from Heaven! It has been so dull until you came."

"We will soon change things and I am sure Princess Zoleka can arrange for us to dance. If there is anyone who can play the piano, we can even dance tonight."

"Why ever not?" agreed Zoleka. "I suppose there is a Music room?"

"Yes, of course there is," answered Udele, "and a large ballroom too, but that is shut up."

"We will find some way to open it," said the Count. "But what we need is someone to play the piano."

As he spoke Anton Bauer came into the room.

"Oh, you are just the person we want," the Count called out before anyone else could speak. "You live here and must know of someone who can play the piano and perhaps even the fiddle. Her Royal Highness and I want to dance."

"You want to dance?" Anton repeated, as if it was something very extraordinary.

"Of course we do. What else is there to amuse one in the evenings?"

Before Anton could respond, the Lord Chamberlain returned and walked in.

They all looked at him questioningly and everyone was silent.

"I have spoken with His Royal Highness," the Lord Chamberlain said to Zoleka, "and he will be very delighted if you will dine with him at eight o'clock this evening."

"And the rest of the party?"

"His Royal Highness of course expects his daughter to come with you, also Count Franz von Hofmannstall and Herr Pieter Seitz."

Before Zoleka could reply to the Lord Chamberlain Udele clapped her hands.

"That is a party, a real party! And it is all so very thrilling."

"Surely there are some *aides-de-camp* in the Palace who should come too," Zoleka asked.

"They are mostly rather old," the Lord Chamberlain admitted, "and although they usually dine with His Royal Highness, perhaps tonight it would be wise if they dined in another room."

He glanced at the Prime Minister as he spoke, who nodded.

Zoleka, now using her Third Eye, suddenly knew the reason. Prince Majmir usually dined with a collection of men of his own age – they just ate and drank because there was nothing more interesting for them to do.

She was as sure of it as if someone had told her.

She thought that Anton Bauer had almost hinted at it when she had questioned him at home.

'I must make sure it is a most interesting evening so that he will ask us again,' reflected Zoleka. 'At least we have jumped a good number of fences on our first day. In fact, if I am not mistaken, the winning post is in sight!'

CHAPTER THREE

They all went upstairs to dress for dinner.

Zoleka walked with Udele into her room first where they found Marla with all the cases unpacked and her bath waiting on the hearthrug.

Udele clapped her hands together.

"Oh, it looks so pretty! It is wonderful that we can sleep in these rooms. I have hardly ever been inside them before."

"Now you are grown up the Palace is yours, Udele. We will make ourselves so comfortable here and tomorrow we will ask for large arrangements of flowers."

"I thinks Your Royal Highness would notice there weren't any," chipped in Marla.

"Come and look at my room and see if it is as nice as yours," Udele suggested to Zoleka.

They walked through to the adjoining boudoir and Zoleka opened the door into the Lily room.

It was a very large room, just like hers, except that the covers and curtains were white and the gilded canopy over the top of the four-poster bed was carved to represent flowers and angels.

"I think you will love this room, Udele."

"It is certainly much prettier than the room I have been sleeping in!"

The housekeeper was waiting to hear their approval of the rooms.

Zoleka said to her,

"Thank you very much for getting the rooms ready so quickly. Tomorrow the Princess and I would like plenty of flowers, I always feel lost without them."

"I will see to it myself, Your Royal Highness," the housekeeper replied.

Zoleka was about to return to her own room when Udele asked her,

"What are you going to wear tonight? I am afraid that all my dresses are very old and shabby. I have not had anything new for a very long time."

"We will go to the shops tomorrow. Meanwhile, as we are about the same size, I will lend you a dress to wear this evening – otherwise you might feel embarrassed."

"If you will be as smart as you look now, I should feel *very* embarrassed, as I have nothing but dull afternoon-dresses I changed into for tea with my governess."

"Comc into my room and let me choose an evening gown for you," suggested Zoleka.

She turned to the housekeeper.

"I would like you to come too so that you can help Her Royal Highness into it."

When Marla heard what was wanted, she produced a most attractive blue gown of Zoleka's, who often wore it when she dined alone with her father and wanted to look pretty but not over-dressed.

Udele was delighted with it.

"When you have put it on, come back and Marla will arrange your hair in a different way. Now you are so grown up, you will have to take a great deal of trouble over it, but I expect there is a good hairdresser in the City."

"There is, and he has come to the Palace once or twice, but only to do the hair of some grand guest who was staying here."

"We will send for him tomorrow and he must think out a new and smart way of arranging your hair."

Zoleka had been told by her father that Udele had Russian blood in her – that was why her hair was dark and so were her very large eyes.

Her complexion was pale and clear and she looked very young.

However, Zoleka was certain that when Udele was dressed up and her hair well arranged she would appear not only more sophisticated, but also extremely beautiful.

She had not appreciated when she first met Udele how striking the contrast between them was.

Zoleka had inherited her mother's golden hair and blue eyes as well as the pink and white complexion which is always associated with English beauties.

But what made her so very unusual was the sparkle in her eyes and the *joie-de-vivre*, which seemed to vibrate from her like a ray of sunshine.

Time was passing and she thought it would be very rude to be late for Prince Majmir.

She hurried over her bath and let Marla choose the gown she was to wear – it was a very pretty one and as it was pink it was a compliment to the Rose room.

She put on her pearl necklace and the two diamond bracelets her father had given her.

She thought when she looked in the mirror that she looked Regal enough and hoped that Prince Majmir would appreciate her.

Udele came running in through the boudoir to join her.

She was looking so totally different from the rather crushed and badly dressed schoolgirl of Zoleka's arrival.

"Look at me! Look at me!" she cried as she came into the room. "Do I not look smart?"

51

"You look very lovely, Udele, and that is how you will always have to look from this moment on."

Udele put her head on one side.

"I doubt it, if I only have one dress to wear."

"We are going shopping tomorrow and no one shall stop us, and then a real fairytale Princess will astonish and delight the whole of Krnov."

Udele was amused by the idea.

When they walked down the stairs together she was talking animatedly.

An *aide-de-camp* was waiting in the hall to escort them to Prince Majmir's private apartments.

He was elderly and Zoleka thought Anton had been quite right in thinking it would be a mistake to have him to dinner with them.

They walked slowly along numerous high-ceilinged corridors until they reached the end of the Palace, where the private apartments of the Prince were situated.

The *aide-de-camp* ushered them into an anteroom where the Count and Pieter Seitz were waiting and for the moment there was no sign of Prince Majmir.

The Count greeted them effusively.

"I was beginning to be afraid that I had lost you both, but now you appear like two angels from Heaven!"

"I am so glad we look like angels," replied Zoleka. "Both Udele and I are hoping for compliments!"

The Count laughed.

"That is what I was just about to pay you. May I say I am so very proud to be dining with two such beautiful young ladies."

Zoleka realised that Udele was looking at him with wide eyes and she was quite certain that this was the first compliment the poor girl had ever received.

Pieter was too much of the diplomat not to add his appreciation as well, so he bowed and kissed the hand of both the Princesses saying,

"I am most honoured to be here tonight at what I believe will be the beginning of a new chapter for Krnov. And who could make it all more memorable than two such lovely Princesses?"

As he finished speaking the door at the other end of the room opened.

Another *aide-de-camp*, even older than the one who had first escorted them into the Palace, announced,

"His Royal Highness is ready to receive his guests."

Zoleka walked towards the door.

They had to cross a passage and into another room where Prince Majmir was waiting.

She was uncertain as what she expected him to look like, but she was not at all prepared for the rather decrepit man who was waiting in the centre of the room to receive them.

His evening clothes did not seem to fit him and his hair, which was slightly grey, was unkempt.

Even before she reached him, Zoleka's instinct told her there was something very wrong.

However, she swept dutifully to the floor into a low curtsy and Prince Majmir bowed to her.

"Welcome to Krnov. I very much hope Your Royal Highness will enjoy being here with us."

"I am certain I shall. It is exceedingly gracious of Your Royal Highness to invite me to your Palace and I am delighted to be your guest."

Then Zoleka presented the Count and she noticed that Prince Majmir was rather surprised to find he was one of the party.

To Pieter Seitz he appeared condescending as if he thought he was of no particular consequence.

It was then that Anton Bauer joined them.

As he seemed a little flustered, Zoleka guessed that he had been making adjustments to the dinner or perhaps rearranging the seating.

Dinner was to be served in Prince Majmir's private dining room next to the room where he had received them.

Neither room was at all impressive – there were no flowers in either of them and the silver on the dining room table was not well polished.

Zoleka was seated on Prince Majmir's right and his daughter on his left with the Count on the other side of her.

They were waited on by four servants, but the fare, Zoleka considered, was not particularly interesting.

She knew her father would not have thought it good enough for visiting Royalty or anyone else for that matter.

There was champagne, but she noticed that before it was served Prince Majmir was given a different drink that was not offered to the rest of the party.

She was wondering what it could possibly be as he quickly emptied his glass and then it was instantly refilled by a footman every time he drank from it.

As Prince Majmir had very little to contribute, the conversation might have been most dreary and boring, but the Count started to amuse them with many stories of the horses he had ridden at home and of races he had tried to arrange without success.

Zoleka realised that Udele was listening rapturously to the Count's tales.

She thought it must be the very first time the poor girl had been allowed to attend a dinner with a young and handsome man – so completely different from her elderly and dull governesses.

'The Count is so right,' she mused, 'we must cheer up the evenings in this dismal Palace or we will all begin to feel depressed.'

As Prince Majmir seemed to have nothing to say to her, Zoleka talked to the others and Pieter joined in with a number of extremely amusing anecdotes.

Course followed course each less imaginative than the last, but the champagne sparkled and on the whole, she thought, the conversation did too.

She politely addressed quite a number of remarks to Prince Majmir and yet because he was so slow in replying, it was usually the Count who answered first.

They had reached the last course and the desert was being served

Turning politely to say a word to her host, Zoleka was aware that his eyes were closing.

She looked at him in astonishment and then to her surprise Anton and the Count rose.

Almost before Zoleka realised what was happening they helped the Prince out of his chair and then they more or less carried him from the room.

She looked at Pieter for an explanation as he told her quietly,

"I had heard before we came here that this always happens in the evening."

"You mean he is drunk?" she asked in a whisper.

"Continually. Now you will surely understand why it is wiser not to dine with His Royal Highness."

"I had no idea!" exclaimed Zoleka, "I never thought of anything like this happening."

Some moments passed before the Count and Anton

returned. They sat down as if nothing had happened and carried on the conversation from where they had left off.

She realised they were being most tactful and were determined to say nothing in front of the servants.

When dessert was finished, Zoleka turned to Anton.

"What is usual here? At home, because my mother was English, the ladies would leave the gentlemen to their port. But in other countries like France there are different ways of behaving."

"As personally I don't care for port," suggested the Count, "I think we should all adjourn to the sitting room where I am sure there will be coffee and liqueurs."

Anton Bauer gave a laugh.

"That would be something unusual, but I will see to it. Princess Udele knows the way to the room which you will be using in the future."

"Is that the one you showed me yesterday?" Udele asked him.

"Yes, Your Royal Highness."

"Oh, that is good. It is a very nice room and I am sure our guests will like it."

"Let us all come with you and see it for ourselves," proposed Zoleka.

They walked back into the other part of the Palace and Udele led them into a room which she said was always used by guests.

It was a beautifully furnished room with many fine pictures on the walls and exquisitely carved gold mirrors – an amazing contrast to the many dreary rooms occupied by Prince Majmir.

Zoleka looked at Anton for an explanation.

"These rooms were decorated for Princess Udele's mother just before she died. She had been complaining for a long time about the Palace looking dull and dismal, and finally Prince Majmir gave in and ordered the decoration of several rooms as a Christmas present."

He gave a sigh before he continued,

"I have always considered it wrong that Her Royal Highness was not allowed to use them rather than the dull nursery upstairs."

"Well, she will most certainly be using them now," asserted Zoleka. "Is there a dining room?"

Anton smiled.

"Yes, there is a small dining room just as attractive as this room and beyond it is what I am sure Your Royal Highness will enjoy – a library."

Zoleka's eyes lit up.

"I was just going to ask if there were books in the Palace. I specially would like to read a history of Krnov if you have one."

"I am sure we have several and, of course, they are all at Your Royal Highness's disposal."

Then the Count suggested,

"I think it is now too late to dance tonight, but I am going to insist that we have some music tomorrow. I have already heard from one of the Officers I have been talking to that there is an excellent pianist in the City and a small band which can be hired any time we require it."

Zoleka laughed.

"You certainly waste no time!"

"I think it is a question of having no time to waste."

She knew exactly what he meant.

However she felt it would be a great mistake to talk openly of their fears about Krnov.

Anton next suggested they played a game of cards and a table was brought in with several packs of cards.

They played ridiculous rather childish games which made them all laugh.

Finally as the clock struck eleven, Zoleka said she thought it was time for them all to retire to bed.

"We have so much to do tomorrow and if the Count is going to keep us up late tomorrow evening we shall need our beauty sleep in advance."

She rose to her feet.

While Udele was talking to the Count, Anton spoke to Zoleka in a low voice so that the others could not hear,

"Would you like to give me your orders now for the morning as I am sure you have a great number."

Zoleka drew him to one side.

"First and foremost, I must purchase Princess Udele some decent new clothes. She only has those childish ugly garments she was wearing when I arrived and tonight she is wearing one of my gowns."

"I thought that was so. There will be no difficulties about it. But how do you want to go shopping?"

Zoleka smiled.

"I think it is important that Princess Udele should become well known in the City and therefore we must go in style."

"With an Escort?"

"Of course."

"It is something that has never happened before," Anton admitted, "and will doubtless cause a sensation."

"That is just what I want."

"And what else, Your Royal Highness?"

"A list, which I am sure will not take much time, of the eligible and interesting young people of the same age as Princess Udele, or not much older, living in the City."

She hesitated before she continued,

"If, as the Count insists, we will be twenty or more for dinner tomorrow night, I would like to see the Chef."

"I cannot think what the Lord Chamberlain will say to all this!" exclaimed Anton.

"I will leave it to you to cope with him, Anton, and some time tomorrow I would like a private meeting with the Prime Minister."

Anton Bauer raised his eyebrows as she carried on,

"It is he who asked me to come here and I think it only right that I should tell him what I am doing in case it is, in any way, contrary to what he wants himself."

"I understand and incidentally I am sorry for what happened tonight. I did suppose that perhaps His Royal Highness would be a little careful as you had just arrived."

"Does he always drink so much?"

"I am afraid so," replied Anton.

"What was he drinking?"

"Vodka."

"Now I understand. My father always told me that vodka suddenly takes possession of you when you are not expecting it."

"I believe that is exactly what does happen to him, but the servants are used to coping with it."

Zoleka gave a heartfelt sigh as she was beginning to understand why no one was doing anything to modernise Krnov.

She said good night to the rest of the party and she and Udele walked up the stairs together.

They had only gone a short way when the Count came running after them.

"I forgot to ask you," he said, "surely you will want to ride tomorrow morning?"

"Of course I do," replied Zoleka, "and if His Royal Highness's horses are disappointing, we will have to ride our own."

"That is just what I was thinking and I have an idea that I would like to discuss with you in the morning. What time can you ride with me?"

"Will eight o'clock be too early or too late?"

"Exactly right and I will get you back for breakfast at nine."

He was just about to descend the stairs, when Udele spoke up,

"Oh, please may I come too?"

"Of course, Udele. We would not think of going without you and I am sure that the Count will ask for an especially good mount for you."

"I promise to do so," the Count called up from the bottom of the stairs, "and we will be waiting for you both at the front door at exactly eight o'clock."

"Thank you, thank you," both Princesses chorused.

As they went up to the landing, Udele sighed,

"I just cannot believe all this is happening. It is so wonderful and so exciting, I am quite sure I am dreaming."

"This is only the beginning," Zoleka told her, "and it is going to get better every day."

When she said goodnight, Udele kissed Zoleka and then hugged her.

"It is so marvellous to have you here in Krnov," she enthused. "*Please*, please do not go away too quickly."

"I will try not to, but my father is missing me and I cannot leave him alone for too long."

She saw disappointment in Udele's eyes and added quickly,

"But do not let us talk about leaving just as I have arrived. We have got so much to do that we must have our wits about us and not make too many mistakes."

"I am sure you never make a mistake, Zoleka. I am already counting the hours I have to sleep before tomorrow morning comes!"

"Hurry up and go to bed. I expect that the maid is waiting for you and Marla is yawning when she thinks I am not looking."

Marla, who had been at the back of the room, piped up,

"It's been a long day, Your Royal Highness."

"I know and you have been so fantastic in getting things shipshape as you always do."

She kissed Udele goodnight again and opened the door into the boudoir.

"Hurry up and go to sleep," she urged her. "It will soon be morning."

"I am just afraid that I shall wake up and find you have disappeared and I am not in the Lily room but upstairs where it is dark and lonely."

"Forget all about it, Udele, and enjoy the Lily room and everything that will happen tomorrow."

"I am quite sure I am going to do so."

She waved her hand and disappeared.

Zoleka closed the boudoir door and walked towards the dressing table.

"What is happening downstairs, Marla?" she asked.

"They feel as if they've been struck by a tornado, Your Royal Highness. The older Palace servants be rather worried in case they've too much to do, but the young ones are a-thinking it's brought new life into the place and not before 'twas wanted."

Zoleka laughed.

"Keep them thinking that way. I am sure they will have to take on more staff if the Count has his way and we throw parties every night."

"His Royal Highness won't be taking much part in them," commented Marla, "from what I hears."

"What have you heard?"

"That he drinks himself stupid every night with two or three of his old cronies and the servants always has to help them to bed as they can't help themselves."

"It's very bad for the country and we shall have to see what we can do about it."

"That'll mean you doing a great deal more than you expects, Your Royal Highness."

"Well, we will have to wait and see, Marla, and you know I shall need your help in getting Princess Udele to look as she should do. I am going to tell the housekeeper that she must have a lady's maid for herself and someone who is experienced."

"I expect that'll be hard to find in this place!"

The way Marla spoke told Zoleka all too clearly she was not impressed with the Palace.

But she thought it was a mistake to say too much.

She was, however, profoundly shocked by what had happened at dinner and she knew her father was quite right in being exceedingly worried about the situation in Krnov.

News travels on the wind and servants always talk and she was therefore certain that the Prince's drunkenness was known all over the City.

That meant not only his own people would know, but so would the Prussians and their local agents who liked to make trouble and therefore prepare the way for taking over the country.

'I shall have to do something about this situation,' Zoleka reflected, 'but I have no idea what the solution is.'

Because it had been such a long day, she fell asleep almost as soon as her head touched the pillow.

She was dreaming, but it was not about Krnov.

*

She was awoken by Marla pulling back the curtains and she could see from the clock by her bed that it was just half-past seven.

The sun was shining and the idea of riding was, for the moment, far more important and more stimulating than anything else.

Having ascertained that Udele had also been called, she dressed hurriedly.

Her riding habit looked very smart and fashionable. With it she wore a small high-crowned hat, swathed with a blue gauze veil which matched the colour of the habit.

Zoleka was well aware as she descended the stairs that the Count was looking at her admiringly as were the other men waiting in the hall.

There was not a sign of Pieter or Anton, but there were three other gentlemen who the Count introduced.

Zoleka realised at once they were Officers from the most eminent Regiment in Krnov and they were young and good-looking.

Udele came running down the stairs a little late.

Zoleka knew that it was exhilarating and delightful for the girl to meet so many young men.

"The Officers are taking us to a place where we can gallop," announced the Count, "and I have chosen a horse for Her Royal Highness which I think she will appreciate."

Zoleka was rather apprehensive in case Udele was

not a good rider, but her mother's Russian blood showed when she was mounted on a horse.

The Officers took them first through the garden of the Palace and out at the back there was a path leading to some plain land which ran alongside the river.

Once there they began to gallop in the high grass and as they did so yellow butterflies flew ahead of them.

The sun was shining and they had a glimpse of the mountains far away in the distance.

It was, Zoleka considered, very nearly as beautiful and enchanting as Opava.

They galloped for a long way.

When the horses began to slow up they were able to talk, so the Count drew his horse beside Zoleka's and they let the others go ahead of them.

"I want to tell you about my idea," he began.

"I am longing to hear it, Franz."

"I walked over to the Officers' mess last night and introduced myself and all they wanted to talk about was horses."

"I am not surprised at that!"

"I also gathered that their Army is very small. The Commander and the Officers I brought with us today are convinced they should expand it and enlist and train many more recruits than they do at the moment."

"I am sure that is just what my father would think is very necessary."

"What I think would be a good idea," continued the Count, "is to say we need volunteers to learn riding from me as an expert and I can be helped by the other Officers if we attract a large number of recruits."

"I think that is an excellent idea, Franz. At least it will increase the number of soldiers guarding the Palace."

"We shall need very many more if we are to protect the whole country."

The Count was talking seriously to her and Zoleka gave him a quick glance.

"What is in your mind?" she asked tentatively.

"I am telling you, Your Royal Highness, that I am extremely worried about Krnov, as I know you are."

"How do you know I am so worried?"

He smiled at her.

"I am not a fool and I realised soon after I arrived in Opava that your father and the more intelligent members of your Government were extremely perturbed about what is happening in Krnov."

Zoleka had not thought that he was aware of this.

As she looked at him in surprise, he added,

"Actually my father talked about it too when I was at home and I realised that something should be done."

"I am so glad you have told me that you feel like this," Zoleka told him. "As I expect you will now realise, I have come to be Lady-in-Waiting to the Princess, not because I wanted to, but because Papa felt it was my duty to help Krnov, as they had asked specifically for me."

She gave a deep sigh and continued,

"Also he is very afraid that the fall of Krnov would endanger the independence of our country and of course of Cieszyn as well."

The Count nodded.

"He is absolutely right. From what I have seen so far I do not believe that Krnov would be able to stand up to any attack from the Prussians."

"Then we must do something quickly. I have asked for an audience with the Prime Minister today. It is he who invited me here, so I know he is worried."

"I suspect that he is as concerned as we are. When you see him, advise him that he must recruit immediately a great number of men into the Army and train them. I will ask for volunteers to learn to ride, but they must also learn to shoot. We can only work as quickly as possible to make them much better prepared than they are at the moment."

Zoleka realised that he was talking commonsense.

"I will do everything that I possibly can, Franz, and I will tell you this evening what the Prime Minister says."

The Count smiled at her, then rode forward to join the other Officers and Udele, and on his instructions, they started galloping again.

It was soon time to return home.

"That was wonderful, absolutely wonderful," Udele enthused when they drew up outside the Palace.

"It is something we must do again tomorrow," the Count suggested, "and may I now congratulate Your Royal Highness on being an excellent rider."

"That is just the nicest thing you could say to me," Udele answered. "I was afraid you would think that I was not good enough for the mount you chose for me."

She bent forward as she spoke and patted her horse.

She looked so very pretty as she did so and Zoleka hoped the men watching her would make a fuss of her.

It seemed so pathetic that she should have spent the last few years since her mother died alone with her father, who was obviously not interested in her.

She had been treated by the staff at the Palace as if she was of no particular importance and like a small child.

Zoleka thought it was extremely unkind of the Lord Chamberlain not to have found playmates for her.

She might even have had girls of the same age to share governesses with her. Instead of which, from what she had gathered, Udele had been doing lessons with dull, middle-aged governesses all alone.

Their only idea of recreation was to take her for a long walk in the Palace grounds and she had been allowed to ride, but only when accompanied by one elderly groom.

No one thought her important enough to require a proper Escort or even an *aide-de-camp* by her side.

'Things will be very different from now on,' Zoleka resolved firmly as they walked into the Palace.

She noticed that although it was nearly nine o'clock there were none of Prince Majmir's *aides-de-camp* on duty and only two footmen to receive them in the hall.

'The whole of this Palace is excessively badly run,' she decided, 'and for that I blame the Lord Chamberlain.'

Her Third Eye had told her last night that he was not at all friendly and now, she felt, he was more likely to be an enemy than a friend.

As she walked up the stairs to take off her hat, she gave a little shiver.

She was beginning to think that with the exception of the Count she was left fighting a lonely battle with not enough ammunition and support to be sure of winning it.

To Udele's delight the Officers took breakfast with them and then they left, saying they were looking forward to riding tomorrow.

"I will require a carriage in half-an-hour," Zoleka said, "to take Her Royal Highness and myself to the shops. Will you please send a messenger ahead now to the most exclusive shop in the City and inform the Manager we are arriving and will require the attention of the Manageresses of all the different departments."

She was making this request to an elderly *aide-de-camp*, who had now condescended to show up.

He gasped at what she had just demanded.

"It is something we have never done before, Your Royal Highness!"

"All the more reason to do it now," Zoleka replied sharply, "and please hurry or they will not be ready for us when we arrive."

The Count was listening to the conversation and he asked Zoleka,

"Anton Bauer told me that you require an Escort."

"Of course."

"I had it mind as well and I think that as the Palace personnel seem not to know their duty, I will send two of your men with you and two from the Palace. It will be the quickest way for them to learn the correct way to behave."

"I think that is an excellent idea."

It was then that Zoleka heard an angry voice behind her,

"It is quite *unprecedented* for Princess Udele, if she goes to the City, to require an Escort."

"Good morning," said Zoleka rather pointedly.

"Good morning, Your Royal Highness," replied the Lord Chamberlain. "I was just remarking that it is quite unnecessary for Her Royal Highness to have an Escort."

"But I am afraid it is necessary for *me*. My father would certainly not allow me to wander about in a strange City without an Escort. In any case, I think, as Her Royal Highness has grown up and no longer in the schoolroom, that people should get to know her and form a deep respect for her."

"And you think that makes it necessary for her to demand a full Escort?" the Lord Chamberlain asked in an aggressive manner.

"I think it is essential and, as I have said, I have no intention of going without one. You cannot be so blind as not to realise that the Princess needs new clothes. She can hardly go on appearing in public in what she has worn in the schoolroom!"

There was nothing the Lord Chamberlain could say.

He was muttering darkly to himself as he stalked away without bowing, as protocol demanded that he should have done to Zoleka.

The Count smiled.

"You will have to get rid of him," he whispered.

"That is just what I was thinking, but I am not sure how!"

"I am sure he will cling to his post as if to a lifeline, which of course it is – no one else would employ such an old grumpy."

Zoleka laughed as she ran up the stairs to change.

*

Once again she had to lend Udele one of her best dresses.

The only clothes she had to wear were childish and so unbecoming, and she knew it would be a mistake to take Princess Udele into the City with what she hoped would be a fanfare of trumpets unless she was dressed for the part.

However, in one of Zoleka's pretty and colourful dresses she looked perfectly presentable.

When they walked down the stairs the carriage was waiting outside the front door.

And so was their Escort!

The two soldiers from Opava looked very different to those from the Palace, although it was obvious that the Count had tried to smarten them up.

Zoleka felt that at least the people in the City would be aware that they were seeing something unusual.

She was not mistaken.

The moment they moved from the park in front of the Palace and into the streets, the children pointed at them.

People walking on the pavement stopped to stare, but Zoleka noticed that nobody waved or cheered as they would have done if she had been at home.

She herself always waved to the crowd and they all waved back and small boys would run beside the carriage trying to keep up with the horses.

It was quite a long way through the crowded streets to reach the shopping centre.

Zoleka looked out from the carriage and hoped that at least tonight the people of Krnov would be talking about their Princess Udele.

The carriage stopped outside a large shop and quite a number of pedestrians stopped to stare out of curiosity.

As Udele and Zoleka climbed out of their carriage, she became aware that they did not know who the young girl might be.

There were no cries of 'good luck'.

Because the Palace messenger had been sent ahead, the Manager of the shop was waiting to receive them.

He bowed politely to Udele and Zoleka and then he asked which department they wished to visit.

"We wish to view your best and smartest clothes," said Zoleka. "Princess Udele is now eighteen and you will understand that she must be dressed appropriately. I am sure that you have beautiful clothes which will enhance her natural beauty."

The Manager gasped.

Despite the word he had received from the Palace, he had not really understood what was required.

Now, almost shaking with excitement, he took the two Princesses straight up to the first floor and sent for the Manageress of each department.

It took them nearly two hours to buy what Zoleka thought was just a foundation of what would be eventually required for her Royal trousseau.

Udele was overcome.

"I never dreamed I would ever own any clothes so beautiful or so many of them," she whispered to Zoleka. "Do you think Papa will be willing to pay for them?"

"I think he will be delighted that you look so smart and pretty."

She thought privately that Prince Majmir might just be difficult at having to pay the bill out of the Privy Purse.

If so, she was sure that the Prime Minister would contribute towards it.

After all to build up the importance of the Royal Family was as important as providing an Army with more soldiers and more guns.

When they left, the Manager of the store, bowing again, thanked them both profusely for their visit.

Even at such short notice he provided two bouquets which he presented to each of the Princesses and promised that everything they had ordered would be delivered to the Palace as quickly as possible.

As they drove away, Udele was rapturous.

"That was fantastic! You do not think Papa will be angry?"

"I see no reason for him to say very much about it. He has to get used to seeing you look pretty and attractive and of course grown up and sophisticated."

Udele laughed.

"He cannot expect me to remain a child for ever."

Zoleka nearly replied that that was exactly what he had done.

Then she told herself that would be unkind, so to change the subject, she said,

"Now we have to wonder who the Count will have asked to dinner tonight. You must wear the prettiest gown we have chosen today for you to make your grand entrance into the Social world."

She only hoped as they drove on that this was true.

Not only did the streets they were driving through look poor and dilapidated, so did the people.

If the Prussians were watching and contemplating taking Krnov over, this would be their moment.

In her heart Zoleka feared that there would be little opposition even from the Krnovians themselves.

CHAPTER FOUR

When eventually they did arrive back at the Palace, Zoleka and Udele had a quiet luncheon with Anton Bauer.

There was no sign of the Count or of Pieter Seitz.

Once luncheon was over there was a message from the Prime Minister.

It said that he would be honoured if Princess Zoleka could come to his office in the Parliamentary building that afternoon.

Zoleka ordered the carriage again and asked Udele to ensure that the Music room was tidy and cleaned for the evening.

"I should also look at the ballroom," she suggested, "in case the Count asks more guests than we expect and do see there are flowers everywhere as it will look very bare otherwise."

The Princess ran off delighted, Zoleka thought, at being able to issue orders at last – something she had not been able to do when she was stuck up in the schoolroom.

The Parliamentary building was not very far from the Palace and on her arrival Zoleka was taken to the Prime Minister's private room where he was waiting for her.

Once he had greeted her effusively and they were alone, he began,

"I do apologise for asking Your Royal Highness to come to me, but I was a little nervous that what we have to say to each other might be overheard in the Palace."

"Who would you suspect might be interested in our discussion?" Zoleka asked him.

She thought for the moment that the Prime Minister was not going to answer, as he might feel it was a mistake to say too much.

Then he answered her,

"I feel the Lord Chamberlain is very hostile to any innovations either at the Palace or in the country."

"I thought exactly the same and, although it may be difficult to contemplate, you should get rid of him."

The Prime Minister made a small helpless gesture with his hands.

"The Lord Chamberlain, as you know, is appointed by the reigning Monarch and I am certain that His Royal Highness will not be interested enough to dispose of him."

"Of course you realise without my saying it that the current situation here is extremely dangerous."

"I realise it only too well, Your Royal Highness. I cannot imagine how they could possibly allow the Army to be run down as they have and apart from anything else the fortifications are crumbling."

"That is just what my father was afraid I might find and if you will tell me exactly how bad it is, he intends to appeal to Prince Vaslov of Cieszyn to help us."

The Prime Minister started and sat upright.

"Prince Vaslov!" he exclaimed, "that is indeed such excellent news. He has achieved so very much for his own country that I believe the Prussians are almost frightened of him."

"If they are frightened of anyone!"

"I am seriously impressed with the Count's idea of recruiting men into the Cavalry, but we do need even more men in the Infantry."

"I think you should talk in detail to the Count about the problem. He seems full of ideas and as he is so young and enthusiastic he will appeal to all of those in the country who are out of work and in consequence feeling hard up."

"That is indeed so," replied the Prime Minister. "I have been worrying as to what I can do about it."

He gave a sigh before he continued,

"The Generals are all old and have no intention of giving themselves any more work. Although I have placed a large order for more weapons, I cannot help wondering who will use them."

This was plain speaking and Zoleka was silent for a moment until she proposed,

"For the time being, until my father can persuade Prince Vaslov to join us, I suggest that you should talk to the Count."

"I will certainly do so," the Prime Minister agreed.

"The Count is also concentrating on cheering up the Palace. We are to have a dinner party tonight and a dance afterwards. I like to think in a way that this might prevent the Prussians from thinking we are particularly worried."

"You are absolutely correct, Your Royal Highness. News from the Palace will carry swiftly over the City and to those outside it."

Zoleka thought for a moment.

"I think I should send Pieter Seitz back to report to my father immediately. I will also ask him to send us more horses, which I am sure the Count will require, unless you have enough here in Krnov."

"Knowing very well how magnificent your father's horses are, I would not think of comparing ours with them and we would be very grateful for any additions to those we already have."

75

"I will pass on the request to my father at once and now please will you help me in another matter."

The Prime Minister looked a little surprised.

"Of course, Your Royal Highness, I will certainly do anything you want."

"There is going to be a very large bill for the new clothes, which Princess Udele simply must have. She must no longer look as if she is still in the schoolroom.

"If the Lord Chamberlain is tiresome, can I send the bill to you? After all, to bring her out as a *debutante* and dress her fashionably as a Princess is, I believe, definitely a weapon against the enemy!"

The Prime Minister laughed.

"Your way of persuading me is quite different from anything I have experienced before. Of course I will cope with the bills, if there is any trouble at the Palace. What you are now doing, Your Royal Highness, is exactly what I have believed for some time is so very necessary for the salvation of Krnov and I am most grateful."

They smiled at each other.

And then Zoleka drove back to the Palace.

*

She sent first for Pieter Seitz.

"As it is such a lovely afternoon," she said when he came hurrying into the room, "I suggest that we walk in the garden."

She recognised by the expression in his eyes that he understood why she was making this suggestion.

"What an excellent idea, Your Royal Highness," he replied. "There are some plants in the garden which I think are very different from ours and your father would be most interested in them."

"They went out into the Palace garden and walked across the lawn towards the fountain.

They were both ostensibly looking at the goldfish and admiring the drops of water falling in the sunshine like a thousand rainbows.

Zoleka told him everything she had discussed with the Prime Minister.

"I suppose you want me to carry the news to His Royal Highness immediately."

"If it is not too much for you, Pieter, as you have only just arrived, but do I think that the sooner Papa knows the situation the better."

"I will go now and tell the Lord Chamberlain, and anyone else who is interested, that because there are going to be many parties you need some jewellery which you did not think you would need."

Zoleka clapped her hands together.

"That is very clever of you, Pieter, and actually it would be useful for me to wear a small tiara and a necklace which Papa thought was too old for me."

"I will bring them back with me, so that there will be no suspicion I was going for any other reason."

"You can tell the Count the truth, but no one else."

"I have already had a long discussion with him this morning. He is extremely worried by the situation."

He paused for a moment as if he was considering what he should say next.

"Last night after you and Her Royal Highness had retired, we went into the City. No one had any idea who we were and we circulated among the men drinking in the bars or talking to each other in the main Square."

"And what did you find out," Zoleka asked him.

As it was such a vital question she glanced over her shoulder as she spoke to make certain that there was no one near them.

"There is no doubt," Pieter told her in a low voice, "that the Prussians are infiltrating the City and the smaller towns. What is more we gathered they are prospecting for minerals in the mountains, which have been left completely unexplored by the Krnovians."

"How can they have been so stupid?"

"That is what happens when there is no one to give orders. You have seen how helpless Prince Majmir is."

"We cannot lose Krnov to the Prussians," asserted Zoleka. "If we lose Krnov they will instantly plan to take over our country and Cieszyn."

Pieter nodded as there was no need for him to say what they both knew was the truth.

"I will go back to the Palace and get ready to leave immediately. I expect you will want to write a note to your father, but make it very discreet just in case I am interfered with on the road."

Zoleka looked at him with startled eyes.

"You do not really think that could happen?"

"I hope and pray it will not."

"Then you cannot go alone! You must arrange with the Count for two of our men to accompany you properly armed."

"I think it would be a wise precaution and of course it would be wise for Your Royal Highness to tell the Lord Chamberlain and anyone else who may be interested why I am returning to Opava."

"Just for a tiara!"

They both smiled a little wryly, knowing how much was at stake.

Zoleka went back to the Palace and joined Udele in organising the rooms for the evening.

They did not see the Count or find out what he was doing until he came in at teatime.

Both Princesses greeted him enthusiastically.

Udele because he was arranging a party just for her which she had never experienced before.

Zoleka because she knew that he was aware of the danger which threatened them.

He was in fact the only person at the moment who could do anything about the problems facing Krnov.

The Count settled himself down into a comfortable armchair and accepted a large piece of iced cake.

"I am so hungry," he remarked, "because I gobbled my luncheon. But I have arranged quite an amusing party for you tonight."

"You really have!" exclaimed Udele eagerly.

"It is *your* party and everyone who has been asked has been told that it is to be the first of a series of amusing entertainments to be given in your honour."

Udele was looking at him with shining eyes.

Then Zoleka said,

"It sounds fabulous. Tell us exactly what you have planned."

"The party tonight will be fairly small as I could not get in touch with all the people I wanted to, but I have arranged for a large formal ball to take place in three days time. The Palace secretaries are sending out the invitations at this very moment."

"A ball for me?" sighed Udele in a rapturous voice.

"All for you," confirmed the Count. "And you are to wear your very best dress, all your jewels and glitter like the fairy on the Christmas tree!"

"I will do it, I promise I will! It is so wonderful I can hardly believe it is true."

"I have also arranged," continued the Count, "that there will be a race meeting next week, which is an event I understand was abandoned by your father five years ago. Fortunately the Racecourse is still there."

He looked at Zoleka as he spoke and his eyes were twinkling.

"I have now engaged a hundred men to prepare the Racecourse and I have instructed the secretaries to send a message to all the people in the country who are known to own horses. If they are not up to our standard, but can use their four legs, that is all I require of them."

Zoleka laughed.

"You are absolutely splendid, Franz. I know there will be a huge response. Everyone, young or old, enjoys a race meeting."

"I have every intention of riding myself and it will be most interesting to find out what opposition I will have to encounter."

"You must not win every race," Zoleka smiled at him, "even if you are heavily handicapped!"

"You are never to mention that word," the Count replied in mock dismay. "Of course I want to win."

"You have to behave like a gentleman and give the others a chance!"

"I am just wondering if I should include a Ladies race."

Zoleka stared at the Count in astonishment.

It was something she had never heard of before, but Udele, however, quickly intervened,

"I want to ride in a horse race. It would be the most thrilling thing I have ever done. Please, please let me take part."

The Count looked across at Zoleka, who made a gesture with her hands.

"It is unusual, but certainly original and it will start people talking."

"That is exactly what we want," added the Count.

There was no need for either of them to say more.

They knew nothing could more attract the attention of the men and women in the street than a race meeting in which women were to take part.

"I have a number of other ideas up my sleeve," the Count murmured. "But I am not going to talk about them at the moment. What I want is to make sure – and this is your department – that we are served better food at dinner tonight than we had last night."

"Oh dear! I meant to speak directly to the Chef this morning. But I will send for him now. Do you want to talk to him too?"

"No, I have a lot of other work to do, but while you are talking to the Chef, Princess Udele shall show me the ballroom. It will be too big for tonight's party, but you did say there was another room."

"The Music room," supplied Udele.

"Then let us go and look at it," the Count suggested rising from his chair.

They disappeared and Zoleka rang the bell.

When the butler came in she told him she wished to speak to the Chef.

"And afterwards I want to talk to you."

He was a middle-aged man who she thought looked intelligent and would understand everything she required. However, she wanted to make sure.

The whole dinner last night had been very slovenly

– the silver had badly needed a good cleaning and the table had not been decorated.

The Chef was with her a few minutes later and to her relief he was a young man and seemed intelligent.

She realised as soon as he spoke to her that he was French, so speaking to him in his own language, she asked how long he had been at the Palace.

"I came here from Paris, Your Royal Highness," he replied. "I am making a tour of Europe staying in different countries to learn their special dishes and also teach them a little about French cooking."

Zoleka smiled.

"Which they certainly need in abundance in Krnov! You might be interested to hear that my father employs a French Chef at home in Opava and the French, of course, know more about food than any other nation in Europe."

The Chef bowed.

"That's so very kind of Your Royal Highness and if I'm allowed to I'll do my very best to please."

"That is exactly what I want to talk to you about."

She quickly found out that up to now he had been very much restricted not only in regard to which food was bought but how it was prepared.

The Lord Chamberlain passed all the Palace menus and invariably he ordered the same dishes over and over again, because that was what he himself preferred.

It did not take long for Zoleka to tell the Chef that she wanted good French cooking and she also told him that he must engage more help because of the parties the Count intended to arrange for Princess Udele.

"That's good news, very good news indeed, Your Royal Highness. I promise you that if I have enough help I can perform miracles."

"You are to engage as many servants as you require and if there is any trouble from the Lord Chamberlain, tell him they were my orders and I will discuss it with him."

The Chef left her, hurrying off to start preparing for tonight's dinner.

Zoleka next had a heart-to-heart talk with the butler to explain that they were planning to invite perhaps thirty of forty people for dinner.

He threw up his hands in horror.

"It's impossible, Your Royal Highness, quite, quite impossible," he cried, somewhat hysterically.

"I am afraid it has to be possible. The guests have already accepted the invitations, which have been sent out in Her Royal Highness's name and, let me tell you, this is to be the first of a great number of parties."

"But I can't do it with the small number of footmen I've got at the moment," he expostulated.

"Then engage more."

"I don't think the Lord Chamberlain will allow me to do so."

"At this very moment," asserted Zoleka, "I am in command. I have come to visit Krnov at the request of the Prime Minister to ensure that this country takes its proper place beside Opava, which is my own country and Cieszyn, which is Prince Vaslov's. I regret to say that you lag very far behind them and are giving a very poor impression to the outside world."

The butler was silent and she continued,

"Either you collaborate and do what I require, or I will find someone who will. It should not be difficult in a City where so many people are unemployed."

The butler, who clearly had no wish to lose his job, climbed down at once

"I'll try and do what Your Royal Highness requires, but it'll not be easy."

"Nothing is easy when things have been neglected and allowed to deteriorate as they have here in the Palace. Employ as many men as you like and I hope tonight at the dinner party the silver will at least be clean and shining, and the very best decorations you keep in the safe must be brought out."

She thought the butler was looking rather stricken.

"May I offer a suggestion? As this is a rush and, as you say, you are short-handed, why not contact the best restaurant in the City and ask them to send you the number of waiters you require? I am sure they would be delighted to come to the Palace, and I will see to it that the Lord Chamberlain pays them appropriately for such occasions."

The butler visibly cheered up.

"I think I can do that, Your Royal Highness, and I know an excellent local restaurant that would be only too honoured if they are asked to help."

"Well, go and see them immediately or send one of your men to do so. There is not much time as the Count has asked the guests to be here at eight o'clock."

The butler hurried from the room.

Feeling as if she had fought two minor battles and been successful, Zoleka poured herself another cup of tea.

She was sipping it when the door opened abruptly and the Lord Chamberlain came bursting in.

He was looking angry and she was not surprised when he said,

"I cannot understand what is happening here, Your Royal Highness, or why so many orders are being given to the staff without consulting me."

"I did not want to trouble you, but the Count has invited, on behalf of the Princess, a large number of young guests to dinner here tonight and has asked me to notify the Chef and of course the butler."

"A large number of guests!" the Lord Chamberlain repeated. "Just how can we entertain them all at such short notice?"

"Quite easily if they carry out my instructions."

"But it is going to cost money and I am certain that His Royal Highness will consider it a totally unnecessary extravagance."

"If His Royal Highness is capable of understanding what is being planned," said Zoleka slowly, "then perhaps it would be wise for me to talk to him. I will explain both why I am here and why it is essential that we should let the world outside be aware there is life in the Palace, and it is not in such a deplorable state as has been widely reported."

The Lord Chamberlain stared at her in amazement.

"I do not know what you are saying. Who has been making these untrue statements about us?"

"Are they untrue?" asked Zoleka. "Surely you must be aware that Krnov is not in any way comparable with the two other Principalities that remain Austrian and free from the Prussian yoke."

She paused, but he did not speak.

"Your people are impoverished simply because you have not developed any of the valuable minerals in your mountains or cultivated the soil properly. Of course the people are poor.

"They do not have enough work and, if you want the truth, your Army is a complete disgrace to any country that wishes to preserve its independence!"

The Lord Chamberlain drew in his breath.

Zoleka knew he was so astounded at being spoken to in such a way that he could not think of an answer.

He would like to drive her away out of the Palace, but that was something he dare not do.

While he fumbled for words, Zoleka continued,

"I think, my Lord, the best thing you can do is to leave me to carry out the work I came here to do at great inconvenience to myself. I have the fullest support of the Prime Minister and I can only hope that, when the Palace does entertain, the guests will not be as shocked as I have been since my arrival!"

As she finished speaking she walked to the door.

The Lord Chamberlain was too astonished by what he had just heard to open it for her.

So she opened it herself and without another word, left the room.

Feeling a little breathless after her outburst, Zoleka walked slowly down the passage to the Music room.

As she expected, the Count and Udele were there rearranging the flowers, which had just been dumped down by the gardeners.

They looked up as Zoleka appeared and the Count observed,

"If you want something done well, you have to do it yourself."

"You can leave the gardeners to me," said Zoleka. "I have just arranged the menu for tonight and the waiters. You will not be at all surprised to hear that we do have not enough help unless we borrow them from the City!"

The Count laughed.

"I rather expected it and I do hope the food will be better than last night."

"I have discovered one good surprise in the whole place, Franz, and that is we have a French Chef."

"That really cheers me up. Do you think this room looks better now?"

Udele had arranged the flowers on the mantelpiece and very artistically around the platform on which the band would sit.

"I think what it wants are palms and aspidistras to stand behind the band as it looks rather bare."

"You are quite right," agreed the Count.

He walked across the room to ring the bell.

One of the footmen answered it after what seemed a little too long for a servant on duty.

"Fetch me the Head Gardener," ordered the Count, "and any other gardener on duty at present and bring them here at the double."

The footman looked startled, but the Count's voice was in itself a command.

They heard him running down the passage.

Zoleka giggled.

"If we go on like this, I have a feeling the whole Palace will fall down on our heads!"

"Nothing would surprise me. I expect the roofing has been neglected and the walls have cracks in them!"

Zoleka laughed again, but at the same time she was well aware it was really no laughing matter.

"Is everything all right?" asked the Count.

"If you want the truth," responded Zoleka, "I think everything here is totally wrong. But what you are doing is marvellous. We can only hope it will make people, whose name we must not mention, pause and think."

The Count nodded and then he said in a low voice which only she could hear,

"We are running against time and that is what really frightens me."

"I know, Franz, we can only hope that we can beat them by keeping one move ahead and by using our brains. Obviously no one in this country has used theirs for a long time!"

"How could they have been such fools?" the Count sighed. "Equally I do love a good battle and this one, my lovely Princess, you and I must win. If we do not, we will never forgive ourselves."

Udele, who was bringing in more flowers, turned round to face them.

The sunshine coming through the window shone on her and she was looking very lovely in one of the dresses she had bought that morning.

It struck Zoleka just how ghastly it would be for her if the Prussians took over her country.

If they did not actually kill her, she would surely be thrown out with her father to live in penury and misery

Into a world where no one wanted them.

Zoleka saw that the Count was looking at her too.

She murmured to him quietly,

"We have to win for *her* sake."

"That is just what I was thinking. She has no one but that drunken father and by the blessing of God, *you*."

"You have forgotten yourself, Franz. No one could have done more than you have done in the last twenty-four hours."

He smiled.

Then in her usual cheerful voice, Zoleka continued,

"And there is a great deal more to come. One thing which is cheap in this country is enthusiasm and one does not have to pay extra for using one's brains."

Zoleka was laughing as Udele joined them.

"This room looks better already," she enthused.

"And it is going to look a great deal better still," the Count added, "when you dazzle them tonight as they have never been dazzled before and they will have so much to talk about when they go home."

"They must thank you and not me," insisted Udele. "How can both of you be so wonderful as to make all these amazing wonders happen?"

"This is just the beginning, but you have got to play your part. You must smile at everyone and make them go home feeling they have never enjoyed a more delightful evening."

"How can I do that?"

Udele sounded a little worried as she spoke.

However, she looked so very pretty gazing up at the Count that Zoleka remarked,

"You are not to be nervous. Everyone coming here tonight will be excited and curious because most of them have never been to the Palace before. What we have to do is to make them think how much they have missed as it is such a beautiful place."

As she spoke three gardeners were ushered into the Music room by the footman.

The Count walked across to them and to Zoleka's surprise he spoke to them in their own language.

He asked which was the Head Gardener and said to him,

"I need your help. Her Royal Highness, Princess Zoleka, has just arrived in Krnov and so have I, to find that the Palace has been neglected and the rooms where we are having a party tonight look dull and dismal.

"The one thing which has favourably impressed me and Her Royal Highness is the Palace gardens."

Zoleka noticed that the Head Gardener straightened his shoulders and looked pleased with himself.

"What I want you to do," added the Count, "may be rather difficult, but I feel you will not fail me."

"What is it, sir?"

"I want you in the next several hours to make the inside of the Palace as beautiful as you have clearly made the garden outside. It means that every flower you have in pots is to be brought in immediately.

"I want aspidistras and palms behind the stage and in the corners of the room which look rather bare, the same in the passages and in the dining room and of course in the drawing room where some of the guests will sit when they are tired of dancing."

The gardeners all gasped before the Head Gardener replied,

"We'll certainly do our best, sir, but I don't think we have enough plants."

"Then do the best you can and for the passages you might have to buy a large number of aspidistras. I am sure you will find a shop in the City which sells them."

"Buy!" exclaimed the Head Gardener.

"I will arrange they are paid for. Just do what you think is right and be as artistic as possible inside the Palace as you have been in the garden. I am sure everyone will be astonished at what they see. And it will be very good for your reputation as a gardener."

The Head Gardener smiled at this comment.

"I wish I'd a little more time, sir."

"You will have more time before the ball that will be given for Her Royal Highness in three days time."

"A ball!" gasped the Head Gardener.

"For that we shall use the ballroom and again I will

require flowers and more flowers. Bring in whatever you can. Buy what is necessary and put on a display which will be talked about the length and breadth of Krnov."

Watching and listening Zoleka realised the Count was putting the Head Gardener on his mettle and he would undoubtedly get his own way.

When the gardeners hurried away to carry out their orders, she cried,

"You are absolutely brilliant, Franz! And I was so very impressed at how well you spoke their language."

"I try never to go to a country before I have learnt its language," the Count told her. "Otherwise I consider it a sheer waste of time."

"Of course you are right. I have learnt the language of Krnov and Cieszyn because I live near them. My father thought it most important for me to learn languages. But somehow I never expected you to be so clever."

"I am not so certain that is really a compliment! I assure you I can speak most European languages, including German."

He gave her a look as he spoke which said far more than words.

"I do think German is a very ugly language," Udele piped up.

"And I think that they are a very ugly people too," added Zoleka. "So we will certainly not ask any Germans to your ball!"

"Supposing no one wants to come?"

Zoleka and the Count laughed.

"I assure you," he told her, "people will already be tumbling over themselves to receive the invitations I am sending out today. You will have to thank the secretaries for working so hard, and also your father's Chief Secretary for knowing the names of all the most distinguished people in Krnov."

"Shall I go and thank them now?"

"I think they would be delighted if you did."

Udele turned towards the door then stopped.

"Do I shake them by the hand?"

"I think it is something they would appreciate," the Count replied, "and something you are going to have to do a great deal in the future."

She smiled at him and ran off.

The Count turned to Zoleka.

"She is very lovely and completely unspoilt."

"We have got to save her, Franz, but Heaven knows how a child of her age and with no knowledge of the world will be able to run a country let alone Krnov."

The Count did not reply and Zoleka commented,

"We can only hope, useless though he is, that her father will not die."

She was about to add, " – *and the Prussians will not arrive too soon.*"

Then she thought that it might be a mistake to say anything in the Palace about that dreaded danger.

She was still thinking of what Pieter Seitz had told her.

It made her shiver and it was almost as if a giant hand was stretching out towards them.

There was nothing to save them from being caught up in it forcibly and crushed by the might and power of the Prussians.

There was only the small effort that she and the Count could make to stop them.

Only if they had enough time could they effectively strengthen and increase the size of the Army and maybe by some miracle they could arouse in the people the will to resist – something they obviously lacked at the moment.

It all seemed so difficult.

Zoleka found herself praying silently in her heart, "*Help us*! Please help us, God!"

CHAPTER FIVE

Looking round the room, Zoleka just knew that the dance was a huge success.

Dinner had been far better than she had hoped and there had been enough hired waiters, so it did not take too long.

The band from the City was small, but they knew all the latest and most alluring tunes.

There was no doubt at all that Udele was enjoying herself. Her brown eyes were shining brightly and she was looking exquisitely beautiful.

The young men were falling over themselves to ask her to dance.

Zoleka gave a sigh of relief.

She had worried so much in case at the last moment everything went wrong, but it could not have been a better evening.

The windows of the dining room opened onto the garden and in some clever way at the last minute the Count had found lanterns to hang in the trees.

There were fairy lights placed around the fountain, which looked even lovelier with the moon rising in the sky and the stars shining overhead.

At one o'clock exactly the Count brought the party to an end.

"Oh, must we stop?" Udele asked plaintively.

"We men have a lot of work to do tomorrow, Your

Royal Highness, and I expect you will find you do too. Do not forget you have a ball being arranged for next week."

"If it is as fantastic as this party, I shall enjoy every moment. Thank you, thank you for being so wonderful."

She looked up at the Count.

"I told you – you would be the belle of the ball."

"Entirely thanks to you and to Princess Zoleka."

He smiled and next instructed the band to play the National Anthem.

Everyone stood to attention and then reluctantly the guests began to say goodnight.

"It has been such a lovely evening," they said one after another.

As the last one left the ballroom, Zoleka turned to the Count.

"I was so afraid it would not come off. But it has all been marvellous. I have come to the conclusion you are a magician."

"That is exactly what he is," agreed Udele. "Ever since you and he have been here the whole Palace has been transformed."

Zoleka looked towards the Count as they were both sharing the same thought.

How long would the transformation last?

As they went upstairs to bed, Udele repeated over and over again how much she had enjoyed herself.

She kissed Zoleka goodnight.

Then childlike she threw her arms round the Count.

"Thank you, thank you! I want to go on saying it a million times."

He kissed her on the cheek and she ran off towards her bedroom.

Zoleka smiled at him.

"No one could be more grateful."

"And I am very grateful to *you*," replied the Count. "The dinner was superb and I expected it to be a failure."

"We have a great many more nights to come when we must succeed as well. So the sooner we both retire to bed the better."

"You are so right. Goodnight and God bless you."

He walked into his room and Zoleka went into hers.

She was pondering at how very charming he was and how intelligent.

It seemed a pity that he was the youngest son as he would not inherit his father's rank or the vast family estate which would go to his elder brother.

'I am sure he will find something interesting to do with his life,' Zoleka said to herself.

Marla helped her to undress and when she climbed into bed she fell asleep immediately.

*

She was woken the next morning by Marla pulling back the curtains and the bright sunshine streamed into her room.

It seemed to her that she could not have slept more than an hour or so.

She then remembered they had arranged with the Count that they would go out riding and it was something she did not want to miss.

Udele must have felt exactly the same, because she was dressed before Zoleka.

She waited and they walked downstairs together.

The horses were outside just as they had been the day before and not only was the Count waiting for them, but four Krnovian Officers.

The two Princesses called out "good morning."

They mounted the horses the Count had chosen for them and they all set off.

Zoleka felt she was enjoying her morning ride even more than she had yesterday.

It was only when they all turned back for home that she found herself riding alone beside the Count with Udele well ahead of them with the Officers.

"Is there any more news?" Zoleka asked him in a low voice.

"Plenty and it is not good."

"What has happened?"

"I sent my valet and another man from Vienna into the City again last night. And I gather from what they have overheard there are a number of Prussians congregating on the Southern border."

Zoleka gave a gasp as she was only too aware that the Southern border was only a few miles from the City and the Palace.

"Do you think they intend to come in imminently?" she asked in a whisper.

"I cannot imagine that they are there for any other reason," replied the Count.

"What can we do?"

"That is what I am trying to figure out."

"It might be a mistake to put a defensive ring round the City in case the people panic, but if we do not do so the Prussians may take over without any opposition."

"You have your men, Franz, and I would suppose the Krnovian Army must be of *some* use."

"I doubt it."

"Then what can we do?"

"I think all that is left is to pray," the Count replied surprisingly.

As if he could not bear to talk about it any more, he spurred his horse forward with Zoleka following him and there was no question of any further private conversation.

They reached the Palace and as she went in Zoleka felt more frightened than she had ever been in her whole life.

The morning had seemed to pass very slowly with Udele having no idea that anything could possibly spoil her happiness. She kept on talking excitedly about the ball and what more they would do to beautify the ballroom.

Zoleka could not bear to tell her that it was unlikely to ever take place.

Most of the dresses they had bought had arrived at the Palace the previous evening and the rest were delivered just before luncheon.

Udele had much to say about her new wardrobe and Zoleka had indeed intended to take her shopping again that afternoon.

There were still a great number of items she needed including colourful nightgowns and underclothes trimmed with lace.

Yet it was beginning to seem so unnecessary when they might have to run for their lives and leave everything behind.

However, there was no point in feeling so miserable until they had to be.

Zoleka forced herself to smile at Udele and respond to her excitement, so they went out shopping again.

On the way Zoleka could not prevent herself from stopping at the Parliamentary buildings where she asked if she could have a word with the Prime Minister.

She left Udele sitting in the carriage, telling her she would not be more than a few minutes and it would not be worth her while coming in with her.

Udele did not protest as she was always amenable to anything that was suggested to her.

Zoleka was taken at once into the Prime Minister's private room and to her relief he was alone.

"I am very sorry to burst in and bother you, Prime Minister, but I had to ask if you had heard the news that the Count told me last night and if it is as bad as it sounds."

The Prime Minister smiled at her.

"I heard your party last night was a great success."

"It really was, but I am now wondering if there will ever be another one."

The Prime Minister put out his hand to touch hers.

"I don't think things are quite as bad as all that, but I have mobilised what there is of our Army and the Count is sending a messenger home to ask his father for help."

"For help! Surely that is a dangerous thing to do."

She thought as she spoke that if the Prussians knew the Prime Minister had become aware of their intentions, they might strike even sooner than they had intended.

The Prime Minister answered her,

"I promise you that we are not going to do anything stupid, nor will we be showing in any manner that we are apprehensive about the Prussians or that we anticipate they are planning any action against us."

"You know of course that they have infiltrated into the City."

"Yes, Your Royal Highness, I have as many men as I can trust watching them. They report directly to me what they overhear and where secret meetings are taking place."

Zoleka smiled at him.

"I can see I am being unnecessarily nervous, but it would really break my heart if Princess Udele, who is at the moment so very happy and thrilled with everything that is happening, finds herself without a country and with no one to support her but her father."

"That is something I am determined to avoid. To be frank I am putting all my faith in the Count. I have never known a young man who is more intelligent and who has more resourceful ideas in an emergency."

"Then we must trust that he will find some way of defending us. Forgive me for coming and worrying you."

"You are welcome to come at any time, Your Royal Highness. In fact, I was hoping you would do so."

The Prime Minister rose as he spoke.

"Go on with the excellent work you are doing at the Palace and make our Princess Udele into a beauty. I can assure you everyone is talking about her."

"That is exactly what I want to achieve."

The Prime Minister bowed to her, kissed her hand and escorted her to the door.

She expected to find Udele waiting in the carriage, but to her surprise she was outside on the grass lawn that encircled the Parliamentary building.

She was surrounded by a crowd of children.

She was talking to them all and two little girls were showing her how well they were able to skip, while a small boy was turning somersaults.

Most of the children had their mothers with them, watching what was happening and obviously delighted that their children should interest the Princess.

When Zoleka and the Prime Minister joined them, Udele enthused eagerly,

"Look how clever this little boy is and the girls tell me they can skip a hundred times without stopping!"

She spoke with much excitement in her voice and the Prime Minister said to her,

"I hear Your Royal Highness can ride better than anyone expected and that you are taking part in a race."

"Is the race really going to be run?" she asked. "If it is, it will be something that has never happened before in Krnov."

"You are introducing us to so many new things," the Prime Minister remarked.

Udele laughed.

"You must thank Princess Zoleka and Count Franz for that idea."

"I am thanking them both and I am glad to see you are making yourself known to our citizens."

He looked around at the children who had stopped playing to stare at him and Zoleka.

"This lady is your Princess," he told them and their mothers, "and as we are so happy to have her here with us, I suggest you give her a cheer and wave to her when she drives away."

The children cheered a little shyly at first and then as Udele climbed into the carriage, they cheered loudly.

They waved and waved as she drove away until she was out of sight.

Udele looked at Zoleka.

"Was it wrong of me to get out of the carriage?"

"No, exactly right, and what you must do whenever you can. Even when I was quite young I always talked to the people who came to the Palace and if I was with Mama in a town, people used to cheer and wave like the children did just now, when we were driving through the streets."

"They do not do that to me."

"But they will in future, Udele. You have to show them that you care about them and that they matter to you."

"They do! Of course they do! But as I was never allowed to pay a visit to the City, I never had a chance of seeing or meeting anyone."

"You are going to have plenty of chances now."

Zoleka hoped as she spoke that it was the truth.

They bought a great number of items to the delight of the shopkeepers including some very pretty high-heeled shoes.

As they drove back to the Palace, Zoleka wondered what had been happening while they had been away at the shops and she could only hope that everything had been quiet and peaceful.

Udele now ran upstairs in order to take off her hat and handed her purchases to her new lady's maid, who had been engaged for her by the housekeeper.

Zoleka as well took off her hat and put it down on a chair and then she walked out through a side door into the garden.

She was feeling, just like her mother had felt when she was worried, that there was nothing more soothing than the beauty of flowers, the soft fall of water in a fountain and the birds fluttering in the trees.

She walked across the lawn.

Among the shrubs there was a small cascade falling from the trees behind the Palace – it flowed down through the garden and into the park that surrounded the buildings.

Zoleka stood gazing at the cascade for a long time.

Then she decided she must go back and give Udele her tea.

She only hoped that the Count would come and join them and she would learn the up-to-date news.

She turned back towards the Palace and as she did so she saw a man coming across the lawn towards her.

She thought for a moment that it must be one of the Officers who had been riding with them earlier in the day.

As he drew nearer she realised that she had not seen him before anywhere.

He was an exceptionally good-looking man, broad-shouldered and taller than most of the men in Krnov.

Zoleka wondered who he could possibly be, as she stood waiting for him to reach her.

She noticed that he was not wearing a hat.

He came nearer still.

She was thinking that he was undoubtedly one of the most handsome men she had ever seen.

He had a square forehead and outstanding features.

She could not tell what nationality he might be.

He was certainly not Krnovian nor did he resemble the men of her father's Kingdom.

The stranger reached Zoleka, smiled and held out his hand.

"I am wondering," he began, "if you are Princess Udele or Princess Zoleka."

He was speaking in Krnovian, but Zoleka was quite sure it was not his mother tongue.

"I was speculating as I saw you approach as to who you were. I am, in fact, Princess Zoleka."

The stranger had taken hold of her hand.

As he touched her she sensed instinctively that he was somehow very different from anyone she had ever met before in her entire life.

She had an overpowering feeling that this moment was of supreme importance.

"Please allow me to introduce myself," the stranger began. "My name is Vaslov and I come from Cieszyn."

"Prince Vaslov!" she exclaimed. "But what are you doing here?"

"I had an idea that I was wanted. I had also heard that you were holding a race meeting very shortly."

"How could you have already heard the news? Did my father tell you by any chance?"

She thought as she spoke that it was impossible as the information she had sent on to her father by Pieter Seitz could not have reached Cieszyn so quickly.

"Your father informed me a little while ago that he was very worried about Krnov, so I have therefore, shall I say, kept a close eye on the country."

Zoleka drew in her breath.

"Then you do realise," she whispered, "how serious things have become here."

"They are very serious indeed and I understand that you have brought a so-called Count with you and I hope you will approve of what I am prepared to arrange with him as soon as I can meet him."

"Oh, please tell me what that is. The Count is very worried, as I am, and we have been wondering frantically what we can do."

"I think I have an answer," replied Prince Vaslov.

"You have? What is it?"

"I have heard of the events that have been arranged for the delight of the Krnovians and I now suggest that you should also hold a Royal Tournament."

Zoleka stared at him, uncertain what he meant and he explained,

"It is what is organised every year in England when the Army gives a display of their ability, not only to march and play their bands, but to use their guns."

"Now I remember! I have heard my father say how interesting the Royal Tournament in London always is and how much it appeals to the people."

"And I think a Royal Tournament will appeal to the citizens of Krnov and will certainly impress those who are peeping over the border."

Zoleka knew exactly what he meant.

"That is what is worrying us all so much."

"I thought it would be and if you can accommodate them, I am bringing three hundred of my best soldiers."

Zoleka stared intently at Prince Vaslov just as if she could not believe what she had heard.

"*Three hundred*!" she repeated.

"There may be a few more if we count in the band, but I want to ask Count Franz where we can pitch our tents and give an impressive performance to the City"

"I think you have just saved us," murmured Zoleka.

"Your father was so right. Krnov needs saving and it is something I should have been aware of before."

"How could any of us have guessed, as we were not invited here, just how bad it is? It was only the new Prime Minister who is aware of what might happen and asked me to come as Lady-in-Waiting to Princess Udele."

"I understand he is a sensible and reliable man."

"That is just what I think as well and the Count has been absolutely wonderful. At the same time the Army is practically non-existent. But if your soldiers are arriving, then I am sure we are safe at least for long enough to make the Army here more efficient than it is at present."

Prince Vaslov smiled at her.

"I think those I am bringing will be most effective, and there are a great number more who can be sent for if it is absolutely necessary."

He glanced around as if he was making sure they were not overheard, before he added,

"It is important that our enemies should not know we are aware of their intentions. I want them to think that what we are doing is just a celebration of Princess Udele's eighteenth birthday. In point of fact she is now, as heir to the throne, the most important person in Krnov."

"How can you be so astute as to know all this?"

Prince Vaslov laughed.

"I keep my eyes and ears open! I am always most curious about what my neighbours are doing, including the very beautiful Princess of Opava!"

At once Zoleka could feel her face reddening at this unexpected compliment.

"Papa has often spoken about you and how brilliant you are, but we have never met before now."

"I was travelling a lot until my father died and now I am determined that whatever happens, the Prussians shall not rob us of our freedom."

He paused for a moment as if he was making up his mind about something.

"I think that I should be frank with you and tell you what my solution really is to the problems of Krnov."

"Oh, please tell me, Prince Vaslov, I have worried so much about it as I cannot see how Princess Udele, sweet and charming as she is, could possibly rule this country of hers alone."

"I am aware of that problem and that is why I have decided to marry her and unite Krnov with Cieszyn! After all our boundaries touch each other."

Zoleka stared at him in sheer surprise.

"You intend to *marry* Udele," she queried slowly.

"I have heard a great deal about her and I am sure she will make a very sweet and admirable wife. In return I will govern this country as well as mine and that will make us perfectly safe from any attempt that might be made by the Prussians."

For a minute it was impossible for Zoleka to speak and then she said,

"Of course if that is what you intend to do, it would certainly be the saving of Krnov. And I am sure that you would do your best to make Udele happy."

"I promise you that I will and now I would like to suggest that I might have the pleasure of meeting my future wife."

"You do understand that she has only just come out of the schoolroom. She has not yet met any men except for the very boring old officials of the Palace until we arrived from Opava.

"Last night was the very first dance she had ever attended and the first party that had ever been given in her honour."

"What you are saying is that I must be very gentle with her and not frighten her in any way. I can assure you that I will not rush my fences where she is concerned."

Zoleka gave a little sigh of relief.

"But you must admit," Prince Vaslov went on, "that it is the logical answer not only for Krnov but for both our countries. If the Prussians take over one of the independent Principalities, they will undoubtedly attempt to incorporate the other two as well."

"That is exactly what my father is frightened they will do!" exclaimed Zoleka.

"So am I. Thus if Krnov cannot rule itself, either he or I will have to rule it."

Zoleka threw up her hands.

"Oh, please, Prince Vaslov, do not give Papa any more responsibility. He has worked so hard for Opava. As you say, your land borders with Krnov and you are young enough to take on both countries at the same time."

"I can but try."

For a moment neither of them spoke.

Then Zoleka remarked,

"I think the Count will be coming in for tea and it is important that you should meet him. You can then ask him where your men can pitch their tents."

"I would suggest as close to the Palace as possible. After all there are two very precious people inside it whom my soldiers are here to protect."

Zoleka realised at once that he meant her and Udele and she smiled at the compliment.

"You are incredibly lovely," he said unexpectedly. "Why have I not met you before?"

"You answered that question when you told me you had been travelling abroad and I was at school. Therefore I did not accompany my father and mother on State visits, including when they stayed with your father in Cieszyn."

The Prince laughed.

"A very convincing answer. At the same time I feel I have been deprived for far too long of someone I should have enjoyed knowing."

He looked at her, she thought scathingly, before he continued,

"I was always told that you are very intelligent and now when I hear what you have done since you arrived in Krnov, I realise what I have missed."

"It is always possible to make up for lost time, but I just cannot understand how you know so much of what has occurred since I arrived."

The Prince's eyes twinkled.

"I have my spies – as you have yours."

"Spys!" exclaimed Zoleka. "Do you mean – ?"

"I mean," he interrupted, "that I have been keeping a very careful eye on Krnov for some time. When I heard you had arrived, I recognised that your father had plunged in while I was still hovering on the brink!"

Zoleka laughed, but he went on,

"I have reproached myself for being so slow and for not having done anything sooner. I promise I will make up for it now and I do believe my performers for the Royal Tournament, when you see them, will impress you."

"You have impressed me so much already and you have given me a delightful surprise, almost as if you had dropped down from Heaven at exactly the right moment!"

The Prince chuckled as they walked into the Palace.

Zoleka led the way to the drawing room where she knew tea would be served.

She was not surprised to find Udele already there talking animatedly to the Count.

When they entered he jumped up and when he saw Prince Vaslov, he gave a cry of delight.

"Vaslov! Where have you come from? I was just wondering whether I should send urgently for you."

"I knew that I would be wanted," he replied, "and I have arrived with a big entourage that I am convinced will delight you."

"What is that?" asked the Count.

"No less than three hundred soldiers to take part in a Royal Tournament!"

The Count gave a shout of delight.

"That is exactly what we need. It is just like you, Vaslov, to turn up so unexpectedly and bring me a lifeboat when I have never needed one so desperately."

"Well, the lifeboat is on its way and there is room for everyone in it!"

Prince Vaslov realised as he was spoke that Udele was staring at him in astonishment.

He turned towards her and bowed deeply.

"You must forgive me, Your Royal Highness, for greeting my old friend Franz before I introduced myself to you."

"I know you are Prince Vaslov and I have always wanted to meet you."

He smiled at her.

"You are meeting me now and you are going to see a great deal of me in the next few days."

Zoleka had moved to the tea table and was pouring out the tea.

She was thinking quickly as she did so that it would be a big mistake for the two men to say too much about the Prussian menace in front of Udele.

As if Prince Vaslov became aware of what she was thinking, he said to her,

"When I heard of the parties you were giving and especially the race meeting, I decided I was not going to be left out."

"I intended to let you know about them," the Count came in quickly, "but I have been so busy the last two days I have hardly had time to think."

"Well, you have time to think now about where you can accommodate my men. Some of them will be arriving late tonight and the rest of them tomorrow morning. They are to take part in the Royal Tournament, which we intend to stage for Princess Udele."

"For me?" Udele queried. "How fantastic! I have never had a Tournament or anything like it given for me before."

"I think you will find it is the first of many," Prince Vaslov told her. "And your people here will be extremely impressed, I hope, at what we are arranging for you."

"It is so very very kind of you, don't you think so, Zoleka?"

"Of course I do, and we are very grateful to Prince Vaslov for arriving just when the Count was beginning to run out of ideas."

"You insult me!" the Count now protested. "I have a great many up my sleeve. But I have always been taught 'one at a time'!"

"You are quite right," Prince Vaslov added, "and as your dance was such a success I am determined not to miss the next one."

"It is such a pity you were not here," said Udele. "It was wonderful, just wonderful! I have never been to a dance before and I enjoyed myself so much I almost cried when it ended."

"As we cannot allow you to cry, I will order my friend Franz to arrange a dance every week for you and, of course, there is nothing to stop you dancing in the Palace whenever you feel like practising new steps and look even more beautiful than you do now."

Udele's eyes widened at the compliment and then she blushed very prettily.

'I feel sure he is clever enough to make her happy,' thought Zoleka.

At the same time she recalled how she had always been afraid of arranged Royal marriages and she had told her father a thousand times he was not even to contemplate one for her.

She intended to marry for love and wanted to be as happy with her husband as her mother had been with her father.

Their marriage had not been arranged. In fact her grandfather had had several young women in mind for his eldest son.

Then her father and mother met by chance one day and fell in love at first sight.

'That is just what I want to do,' she told herself.

She wondered if by any chance Prince Vaslov had fallen in love with Udele as soon as he had seen her.

She was looking exceedingly pretty in an attractive pink gown that enhanced the darkness of her hair and the whiteness of her skin.

There was no doubt, now she was properly dressed, that she was a very beautiful woman.

Of course she was still very young – she had been kept in the schoolroom and not allowed to meet people.

She still had the simplicity and unselfconsciousness of a child and Zoleka felt sure this must appeal to Prince Vaslov.

Equally from what she had already heard about him and from what she felt instinctively, he was a most astute young man.

He must, she calculated, be getting on for twenty-seven and he had seen a great deal of the world.

She had always been told that the conversation at the Court in Cieszyn was not only interesting but unusual, quite different from the chitter-chatter so very common in most Palaces.

'Will Udele be able to cope with all that?' Zoleka asked herself.

Then she remembered again that Prince Vaslov was very clever and that he would realise at once that he would need to teach his wife what he wanted her to know, as well as to make her interested in what interested him.

'If he does so with love as well as wisdom,' Zoleka thought, 'they will be very happy together.'

Then she looked at the Count and saw that he was frowning and she wondered what was worrying him.

Nothing could be better than for Prince Vaslov to have appeared and bring three hundred soldiers with him.

She felt it unlikely if the Prussians were planning to take over Krnov, they would risk a pitched battle.

She was certain, from what she had heard, that their tactics would be to encroach gradually and subtly into the City of Krnov and at a given moment they would take over the Parliamentary buildings and the Palace.

Members of the Krnovian Government would be shot or imprisoned and there was every likelihood of their doing the same to Prince Majmir and his daughter.

They would receive little support from their people and at the very least they would be exiled from Krnov and their very existence forgotten.

Zoleka's Third Eye told her that this was what was being planned.

She thought it would be the obvious policy for the Prussians to adopt without Krnov's neighbours being even aware of what was happening.

Now that Prince Vaslov and his men had arrived, Prussian strategy would not be as simple for them as it had been.

She was almost certain they did not have enough

troops nearby to cope with any other country except for Krnov.

They would expect little or no opposition from the Krnovian Army or from the citizens themselves.

There were only two paths the Prussians could now take, Zoleka worked out.

The first was to build up a much larger force for the invasion of Krnov and that would undoubtedly take time.

The second was to abandon the idea altogether for the moment which would certainly be the most satisfactory from Krnov's point of view.

But she knew how greedy the Prussians were.

They desired the coal and other valuable minerals which lay in the mountains.

If Udele was to make Krnov prosperous, she would undoubtedly need a husband, as only a man could lead the country as it should be led.

Zoleka was worrying again about the uncertainty of arranged marriages and she remembered that all too often they proved unhappy.

Looking at Prince Vaslov now, she felt that Udele was very lucky as she would be married to a strong Prince who would make Krnov as rich and prosperous as he had made his own country.

Having met so few men, Udele would undoubtedly fall wildly in love with him.

'It would be most difficult not to,' mused Zoleka, 'considering how good-looking he is and what a charming way he has of speaking.'

He was talking to Udele now and obviously paying her more compliments.

She was not only blossoming like a rose at hearing them, but she looked attractively shy.

'That blush on her cheeks would entrance any man, young or old.'

Zoleka rose from the table.

"I hope that Your Royal Highness will dine with us tonight," she asked, "and how many of your entourage will you be bringing with you?"

There was a pause before the Prince replied,

"I would like to know first whether I am invited to stay in the Palace."

"Indeed you are. I never considered anything else. And let me tell you again how very glad and privileged we are to have you with us."

"I will add to that," said the Count. "Only a genius would have thought of bringing so many men here to stage a Royal Tournament that has never been heard of in Krnov before."

"Everyone will be very thrilled," cried Udele. "Just as they will be thrilled with the races which have not taken place for years."

"I intend to win every one of them!" Prince Vaslov boasted.

Udele gave a little cry.

"You must not do that. It is the Count who thought of the idea and naturally he wants to win the big race."

"What prize are you giving to the winner?" Prince Vaslov enquired of the Count.

"I had not thought about it, but as a distinguished visitor I think it should be your contribution."

"Ask a silly question and you get a silly answer! All right, Franz, I will give you a Gold Cup or whatever you want. But I shall be extremely annoyed if you beat me to the winning-post!"

"I shall be doing my very best!"

Both men were laughing and Udele said to Zoleka,

"Oh, this is so exciting! Please can we dance again after dinner?"

Zoleka glanced at the Count.

"Did you hear that request?"

"I did, but unless Vaslov is going to produce some ladies for us, the four Officers he is bringing to dinner will have to dance with each other!"

Zoleka thought for a moment before she proposed,

"I think it would be an anti-climax after the success of last night's dance. I am sure we can play card games or better still to gamble, which will be a different amusement. Then tomorrow night I will invite some pretty young ladies to please you."

They all agreed to her suggestion.

Then the Count took Prince Vaslov away with him to show him where his men could pitch their tents and he also wanted to introduce him to some of his Officers who were teaching the recruits to ride.

"What I really want to see," Prince Vaslov enquired as they left the room, "are your horses."

"I am certain he can," Zoleka murmured to Udele. "It is a pity the horses cannot dance otherwise they could come in after dinner!"

Udele thought this was very funny and she slipped her arm into Zoleka's.

"Please come and tell me what gown I should wear tonight."

"Of course I will and I am sure you will find Prince Vaslov very charming and you will want to look your best for him."

There was silence for a moment as they reached the bottom of the stairs.

As they walked upstairs, Udele remarked,

"He is nice and very good-looking, but rather old. I like dancing with Count Franz and would rather dance with him than anyone."

CHAPTER SIX

The French Chef was now well into his stride and the dinner was delicious.

Afterwards Prince Vaslov's Officers said they must go to see that their men were comfortable in their tents that they had been so busy erecting ever since they had arrived and the Count had insisted that they should be in the Palace grounds.

Udele was rather frightened in case it annoyed her father.

"I am quite certain he will understand that we need the soldiers near us," Zolcka soothcd hcr.

As she spoke she gave the others a warning glance that they must not let Udele know that they were there to protect her against the Prussians.

She still had no idea of how worried everyone was about the present situation.

The two Princesses and the Count went to sit in the drawing room.

Anton Bauer kept coming in and out to report what was happening and any likely developments.

"They all have comfortable tents," he said, "and the men seem satisfied with them. Prince Vaslov had asked if his Officers can occupy rooms in one of the wings of the Palace and with some difficulty the Lord Chamberlain has eventually agreed."

"As the Palace is as good as empty," commented Zoleka wryly, "he can hardly say there is no room!"

A little later Prince Vaslov returned to confirm that he was delighted with all the arrangements.

"What I have come to tell Princess Udele," he said, "is that she is to receive the band when they march into the City tomorrow with three hundred soldiers behind them."

Zoleka's eyes lit up at the proposal, but Udele was looking nervous.

"It is wonderful that we shall have a band, but how do I receive them?"

"I am arranging," replied Prince Vaslov, "that you will be reviewing my soldiers from a platform in the main Square. They will march through the City and form up in front of you and then you will say a few words to them."

Udele gave a little cry.

"But what shall I say to them? I have never made a speech in my life."

"Then it is time you learnt. All you have to do is to thank them for coming to visit Krnov, say just how pleased everyone is to have them and that you are looking forward to the Royal Tournament."

Udele still looked frightened as the Count added,

"I have been sending my men all over the City to tell people about the Royal Tournament. I am quite certain the news will spread like wildfire and everyone will want to be present."

"I think the site you have found for the ceremony is excellent," remarked Prince Vaslov.

"It wants a lot of tidying up and some repairs, like everything else in this place, but it will seat a large number of people and there is plenty of room for those standing to see what is happening."

Prince Vaslov smiled at Zoleka.

"You see," he muttered, "when you have two men to

arrange matters and who know exactly what they want, everything falls into place!"

"I am full of admiration for you both and please do not worry about your speech, Udele. I will write it down for you and you can learn it by heart."

"Oh, thank you, Zoleka! I am certain that you have made plenty of speeches, but the only person I have had to talk to has been a governess."

"Well, where you had one person, now you have a cast of thousands," Prince Vaslov intervened, "and every one of them thinking how wonderful you are."

"Will they really think that? Perhaps they will be disappointed in me."

The Count jumped up.

"I will tell you what they are going to see."

He took Udele by the hand and took her across the room to a long mirror in a gilt frame hanging on the wall.

"Now look into this magic mirror and tell me what you see."

Udele obeyed him.

"I only see me!"

"Exactly!" answered the Count. "And that is what your people and remember they are *your* people, are going to see tomorrow. Someone very lovely, very smart and, of course, someone who loves them."

Udele gave a little laugh.

"Now you are teasing me, but I will try to look all of those things."

"You look them all now," he asserted. "And that is why you are going to delight the whole of Krnov as it has never been delighted in its history."

Listening Zoleka thought he was being very clever

with her as it suddenly struck her how strange it was that they had not seen Prince Majmir since the night of her arrival.

Very quietly, while Udele was talking to the Count, Zoleka asked Prince Vaslov,

"Have you any idea how His Royal Highness is?"

"I imagine he is quite happy drinking in his rooms," he replied scornfully, "and is totally oblivious of what is happening. I believe the only one who sees him regularly is the Lord Chamberlain."

Zoleka mused that meant there were two unpleasant people together, but decided not to say so.

"As we have a lot to do tomorrow," she suggested, "and Udele must learn her speech before she goes to sleep, we are retiring to bed. I propose that you two men, after all the work you have done today, do the same."

"We will try and obey you," smiled Prince Vaslov, "but first I want to show Franz something very new, which I have invented for alerting my men if there is any danger."

"Why should there be any danger?" asked Udele in an alarmed voice.

"Even soldiers have accidents with their guns and their horses," Zoleka said quickly, "and it is very sensible of Prince Vaslov to think about it."

She gave the men a warning glance before they said goodnight.

She and Udele went upstairs.

"It will be wonderful to hear a big band playing," Udele was saying as they reached their bedrooms.

"I am looking forward to hearing them too, now let me write down your speech for you. If you read it aloud, two or three times before you go to sleep, you will find you will remember every word in the morning."

She went into the boudoir and Marla followed her.

It only took her a few minutes to write down what she thought Udele should say and it was very much along the lines that Prince Vaslov had suggested.

"I will say it over and over to myself, Zoleka. I do not want you all to be ashamed of me."

"We shall never feel that, Udele, and now you are so important, you may have to make a number of speeches. But do not be frightened. Just remember that people want to hear your voice and listen to what you are telling them."

"I will remember and I only hope it's true."

She gave Zoleka a big hug.

"You are so incredibly kind and marvellous to me. Everything has changed since you arrived in Krnov."

"And it will continue changing and always getting better and better."

Zoleka only hoped as she spoke that what she was saying was true, but she had to admit to herself that things were very different from when she had arrived.

Dinner tonight at the Palace had seemed even more enjoyable because Prince Vaslov had been present.

Zoleka found him more interesting every time she spoke with him and she could certainly believe that he was an outstanding Ruler of his own country.

What she found rather strange was that, when they were talking or arguing with each other, she felt she could read his thoughts.

And she had a suspicion that he could read hers.

'Perhaps he too has a Third Eye,' she thought, 'and it is really something very unusual.'

When she climbed into bed she was still thinking about him and she strangely found herself looking forward to tomorrow and being with him again.

He was surely the most attractive and singular man she had ever met.

*

Prince Vaslov had arranged for them to arrive in the Square at ten o'clock exactly and this meant that they had to drive from the Palace dressed in their very best clothes.

Zoleka chose a lovely green dress for Udele and a hat which did not hide her face, but she had wanted to wear one of the larger hats they had bought which was certainly very pretty.

However Zoleka told her firmly,

"It is always a big mistake for Royalty not to show their faces. The one I have therefore chosen for you will make it possible for everyone to see your eyes."

"I would never have thought of it, but I will always remember everything you are teaching me, Zoleka."

Udele looked very lovely and most attractive when they walked downstairs so that even the elderly *aides-de-camp* glanced at her admiringly.

The Lord Chamberlain, however, was disagreeable as usual.

He was, Zoleka knew, absolutely appalled at what was taking place both in the Palace and outside.

The Count had said gleefully,

"He nearly had a fit yesterday when we told him all the Officers from Cieszyn were to occupy the left wing."

"I think he is a horrible man," Zoleka added. "But the Prime Minister says it is almost impossible to get rid of him."

"Then we shall just have to ignore him. He tried to threaten me today that if I brought more Officers into the Palace he would refuse to accommodate them."

"Can he do so?"

"Not without Her Royal Highness's agreement now she has taken over!"

"Then we should not worry. She has never been so happy or allowed to enjoy herself as she is doing now."

"That is just what I want to hear. After all it is her country and the very first person who should be happy here is Udele."

She was certainly excited as she and Zoleka turned towards the Square with an escort of Cavalry.

They were travelling in an open carriage drawn by four horses.

Anton Bauer and Pieter Seitz, who were with them, were dressed in their best and most impressive diplomatic uniforms.

Prince Vaslov and the Count rode at the front of the Escort, looking exceedingly smart in full military dress and feathered hats.

While they were driving through the streets throngs of people rushed to look at them and when the carriage had passed by they followed behind.

When they reached the Square it already seemed to be crowded.

An area had been cordoned off where the band and the soldiers could form up when they arrived.

As they climbed onto the platform they could hear drums in the distance.

There were seats for the Princesses on the platform, which had been decorated with the colours of Krnov.

There were even, Zoleka noticed with a smile, large arrangements of flowers.

She and Udele were presented with large bouquets when they arrived by the Prime Minister and the whole of the Krnovian Cabinet was seated behind them to watch the proceedings.

As the Prime Minister greeted Zoleka, she said to him in a low voice:

"This is what we have hoped and prayed for."

"Exactly, Your Royal Highness, and I am so deeply grateful to you."

"You must thank Prince Vaslov as well for arriving at the very moment he was wanted."

"An inspired answer to our prayers," affirmed the Prince Minister warmly.

The band came nearer.

Now everyone was alert and looking towards the street along which they could enter the Square.

When they rounded the corner they appeared most impressive. Every bandsman was wearing a red coat and a particularly striking headdress.

They were playing a rousing march which seemed to echo and re-echo round the Square as they entered it.

They marched precisely and very smartly and they formed up into their positions facing the platform.

The soldiers behind them marched in even ranks to stand to attention beside the bandsmen.

After a poignant pause the band played the National Anthem of Krnov.

It was a gesture, Zoleka thought, which only Prince Vaslov would have thought of making.

As they all stood to attention she felt everyone was moved – not only by the music, but by Princess Udele who was standing in front of the dignitaries on the platform.

As the Krnov National Anthem ended, the soldiers presented arms.

Then to Zoleka's delight Udele made her speech.

She spoke slowly as she had been advised to do and she pronounced every word carefully.

There was complete silence until she finished and as she smiled, the people of Krnov went mad.

They cheered, shouted and waved.

They appeared to be entirely different from the dull, apathetic people Zoleka had seen earlier in the streets.

It was, in fact, so emotional that there were tears in her eyes as well as Udele's.

Their Princess waved back at them and as the Prime Minister stepped forward to join her on the platform, the cheering died away.

He made an excellent speech.

He welcomed Prince Vaslov to Krnov and thanked him for the pleasure he was bringing to the citizens of their country.

He also informed his audience that Princess Udele was now grown up and since her father Prince Majmir was unwell, she had taken over as the Ruler of Krnov.

They could look to her for new developments, new interests and a reign of prosperity such as they had never seen before.

There were more loud cheers as the Prime Minister sat down and then the band struck up a popular tune.

Next the soldiers from Cieszyn began to march and counter-march in a way that Zoleka had never seen at any military parade at Opava – her father had told her it was very much part of the Royal Tournament he had watched in England.

It was over two hours later before they were able to drive back to the Palace.

The people cheered as they passed them and small boys ran beside the carriage.

Prince Vaslov and the Count next led the band and all the soldiers to show them where the Royal Tournament was to take place and afterwards the Officers came into the Palace for luncheon.

When they had all enjoyed a drink in the drawing room, it was a very cheerful party which moved into the dining room.

Everything at the Palace was now so different from when Zoleka had arrived.

The butler with his new footmen had the best silver on the tables and there were enough waiters for them to get through the meal reasonably quickly.

"We have a great deal to do this afternoon," Prince Vaslov was saying. "Once all my men have settled in they have to rehearse to attain the perfection we wish to show to the public."

"If I did not know you so well," the Count chipped in, "I should have thought it impossible. But after what has transpired today, I believe that everything you touch turns to gold."

Prince Vaslov laughed.

"I only hope you are right, Franz, but events have turned out even better than I could have hoped.

He turned towards Udele.

"Your speech was so perfect, Your Royal Highness, I cannot believe it is the first speech you have ever made."

"Was I really all right?"

"You were quite perfect," added the Count. "And you looked exactly as you did when you saw yourself in the magic mirror."

Udele blushed and then she turned to Zoleka,

"If I was rich, I would give fabulous presents to all you fabulous people. But I think Papa would be angry. So what can I do?"

"You have given us a present by doing exactly what we were hoping you would do, Udele, but we will think of something, although I cannot believe Prince Vaslov wants for anything."

She was speaking lightly and then she remembered that he had told her he intended to ask Udele to be his wife.

As the thought surged into her mind, she looked at him instinctively and knew he was reading her thoughts.

Then to her great surprise an expression came into his eyes which she did not understand.

Yet for some reason she could not explain, it gave her a strange feeling inside her breast.

It was something she had never felt before in her entire life.

For a heart-stopping moment it was impossible for her to look away from him and as she finally tore her eyes away from his, the Count said,

"Come on, Vaslov, we must get down to business. I suppose you realise that in a day or so we are giving a ball and I have not yet finished all the arrangements."

"I will help you," he promised, "and if there is one thing I shall enjoy, it will be dancing with our very clever little Princess."

He looked towards Udele as he spoke, but she had run to the Count's side.

"Please, please can we have a cotillion? I have read about them in books and it would be very wonderful to have one at my ball."

"Of course you can have one," the Count answered. "But it means that you and Zoleka will have to buy a lot of presents, otherwise those who take part in the cotillion may be disappointed."

"We will, of course we will. I think it will be so thrilling."

The Count smiled.

"I can think of many other excitements for you in the future, but you will certainly have your cotillion."

"Oh, you are so kind."

In the same childlike way Udele had done last night she threw her arms round the Count and kissed his cheek.

"That is just the present I want from the cotillion," he sighed. "But it must be exclusive to me and not given to anyone else!"

"No, of course not. After all no one else has done for me what you and Zoleka have."

The men hurried away and Udele started to talk to Zoleka about what they should buy for the cotillion.

Zoleka thought it would be an anti-climax for her to appear shopping in the City so soon after the grand pomp and circumstance of this morning.

So she sent Anton Bauer to ask some shop-keepers to bring a selection of presents to the Palace for the cotillion.

Zoleka then sat down on a sofa in the drawing room and put up her feet.

"I am going to rest. I think I deserve it."

"Of course you do, I will go off now and talk to the gardeners about the flowers we will need to decorate the ballroom."

Udele hesitated before she added,

"I know Count Franz has told them what to do, but I thought it would be so pretty if all the flowers round the bandstand were pink."

"That is such a splendid idea! Go and tell the Head Gardener that is what you want."

Udele hurried away and Zoleka thought that it was very good that she was beginning to think for herself.

She was even prepared to give orders to the Palace servants, which had never been allowed in the past.

Zoleka was feeling very tired and it was more from worrying about the Prussians than from physical exertion.

She closed her eyes and a few moments later was fast asleep.

She was dreaming of Prince Vaslov, his band and his columns of marching soldiers

And when she opened her eyes, she found that he was standing by the sofa looking down at her.

"I am afraid I have been asleep," she murmured.

"You look so very lovely as the Sleeping Beauty – lovelier than any woman I have ever seen in my life."

She glanced up at him in surprise.

He sat down on the edge of the sofa.

"I am worried, Zoleka," said Prince Vaslov.

"Why?" she asked.

She was surprised he had used her Christian name as they had been rather formal to each other since he had arrived.

"I have never met anyone like you before and there have been a certain number of women in my life, I do not pretend there have not been, but *you* are different."

It was just what Zoleka was thinking about him.

Yet she did not know what to say to him now.

She looked shyly at him and she could see that he was rather embarrassed because she was blushing.

"You are so incredibly lovely, Zoleka, yet I do not believe there have been many men in your life."

She gave a little laugh.

"I have been very happy with my dear father. We entertain so many people in Opava, but they are mostly his age, not mine."

"Yet you have been brilliant enough to completely reorganise this Palace and transform Udele, as if you had waved a magic wand."

"If she is guided in the right way, she is going to be a charming young woman and a very successful Ruler."

"I do realise that, but what am I to do about *you*?"

Zoleka's eyes opened in surprise.

"What do you mean?"

"I do not have to explain to you – you know exactly what I mean."

For a moment there was silence.

Then without saying anything further Prince Vaslov rose to his feet and walked out of the room.

As the door closed behind him, Zoleka put her hand to her breast.

She was in love.

As she thought about it she was aware she had been in love with him from the moment she had first seen him.

But she had not realised that it was love.

She only knew that he was the most handsome and exciting man she had ever met.

It seemed strange that she could read his thoughts as he could read hers.

There was something inevitable about it all.

But Prince Vaslov had come to Krnov determined to marry Udele as it was the only way they could save the independent Principalities from the Prussians.

*

Prince Vaslov did not return for tea, although the Count put in an appearance, but only stayed for a while.

He said they were terribly busy with the band and making all the final arrangements for the next contingent of soldiers which had just arrived.

131

"It seems incredible," he said to Zoleka, "that two days ago we were complaining we did not have anyone to protect us and now we have almost too many!"

"You cannot be sure," she answered in a low voice. "After all, we do not know the number of Prussians there are in the City or how many are waiting across the border."

"I am aware of the problem and I assure you we are taking every possible precaution. That is why I am posting every man I can around the Palace."

"Do you think the enemy need to hold the Palace in order to assert their authority?" asked Zoleka.

"But of course. They will undoubtedly wish to be rid of Krnov's present Ruler, whatever condition he is in."

The presents for the cotillion duly arrived from the shops.

Udele enjoyed sorting them all out and buying what she considered the most attractive until finally she decided that she had selected enough.

Then she and Zoleka recognised that the bill for the presents would have to go to the Lord Chamberlain.

"I am too frightened to ask him," admitted Udele. "If he says no, what shall I do?"

"It is not such a great sum, but *I* will speak to him."

Zoleka told one of the Palace *aides-de-camp* in the hall that she wished to speak to the Lord Chamberlain.

A quarter-of-an-hour later he came to the drawing room and one look at his face told Zoleka how much he disliked her.

"I am sorry to bother you, my Lord, but Her Royal Highness has now chosen all the gifts we require for the cotillion which will take place at her ball. I thought it only polite that I should present you with the bill rather than that you should receive it directly from the shop."

"Cotillion! What cotillion?" the Lord Chamberlain enquired.

"You must be aware that the Princess is very young and this is the first ball she has ever had given for her. She has asked for a cotillion, and, of course, we want her to be as happy as possible and to enjoy the first party at which she has ever been the hostess."

"I should have thought you have had enough parties these last few days to last a lifetime," he snapped.

"Are you now referring to your lifetime or Princess Udele's?"

"We cannot afford to spend any more money," he shouted aggressively.

"In that case I will have to ask the Prime Minister. But I thought that was rather humiliating for such a small sum. However if you do not mind, it does not trouble me!"

The Lord Chamberlain threw up his hands.

"I want to know what is happening here. What are all these soldiers doing and why are there so many Officers staying in the Palace without my permission?"

"You can scarcely refuse them considering they are here to save you and Krnov from being taken over by the Prussians."

"Taken over by the Prussians?" he expostulated. "I have never heard such silly nonsense. They are thinking of no such thing."

"Then I suggest you talk to Prince Vaslov, who has come here specifically to save the independence of Krnov. If you are not worried, then I assure you anyone with any brains is terrified at what is likely to happen."

The Lord Chamberlain stared at her.

"I just don't believe it."

"Go and talk to the Prime Minister. Or better still,

allow Prince Vaslov to tell you just what he and my father think about the way this country has been so mismanaged. You are on the verge of losing your independence and that, of course, must endanger both Opava and Cieszyn."

"I think you are talking a lot of nonsense," the Lord Chamberlain spat angrily. "If you are so frightened of the Prussians, you should go back to your own country where you will doubtless feel quite safe."

He did not wait for Zoleka to reply, but stalked out of the room slamming the door behind him.

She gave a sigh.

Then she remembered the bill for the presents.

If it was not met by the Lord Chamberlain, Prince Vaslov was rich and he would obviously be pleased to pay it for the girl he wished to marry.

Even as the thought came into her mind, she felt as if she was suddenly stabbed in her heart by a sharp knife.

'How can I be such a fool,' she asked herself, 'as to love a man I have only seen two or three times?'

Then she knew that this really was the love she had always wanted to find.

The love that united those who found it so that they became one rather than two people.

'How *can* I love him? How can I love him?' she asked herself over and over.

But she knew that she did.

*

It was very difficult for her to go down that evening to dinner and behave naturally.

She did not dare to look at Prince Vaslov in case he could read her thoughts.

She had rearranged the dining room table so that he was not sitting next to her.

Because there had been so much to do most of them around the table were very tired and the Officers who had just arrived made an excuse to leave the party early.

But Prince Vaslov seemed to have plenty to say and seemed unperturbed by what was going on.

Zoleka thought that he was even cleverer and more interesting than he had been last night.

Finally as their numbers had been reduced, she said that she was retiring to bed.

"I have been working out a plan for Princess Udele to drive through the City tomorrow morning," announced the Count, "to inspect the Racecourse."

"Oh, I would love to do that," cried Udele.

"Then if things are a little tidier than they are at the moment, you shall go to see where the Tournament is to take place."

She was very taken with this new idea and Zoleka almost had to drag her away to bed.

After she had kissed Udele goodnight, she walked to her own room and after Marla had helped her to undress, she climbed into bed without saying anything.

It was only when she was alone in the dark that she could dwell on Prince Vaslov and how handsome he was.

'I love him! I love him!' she admitted to herself.

She was wondering if she could possibly remain in Krnov and be present when he married Udele.

She must never betray the fact that it would break her heart.

'How and *why* has this happened to me?'

People had asked this very same question since the beginning of time.

But it had happened and her love was throbbing in her heart and in her soul.

Finally she fell asleep and dreamt of Prince Vaslov as she had seen him the very first time, walking towards her in the garden.

Then suddenly she awoke and opened her eyes.

The room was in darkness except for the moonlight streaming in through the sides of the curtains.

Yet she was aware that something was wrong.

Something that was very very dangerous.

She could feel the threat so strongly that she knew it was not her imagination.

It was her instinct and her Third Eye was speaking to her urgently.

Danger was close and coming nearer and nearer.

'It just cannot be true,' she tried to say.

Without thinking what she was doing, she climbed out of bed and walked to the window.

She pulled aside the curtain.

Her room and Udele's looked out over the garden.

The moonlight turned the water in the fountain to silver and the garden itself looked enchanting.

Then as she stood staring down, she became aware of a movement on one side among the bushes.

At first she felt certain it must be the wind and then she could feel at the open window that there was no wind.

She looked again at the bushes.

Faintly touched by the moonlight, she realised that someone was moving through them.

Not one person but several and they were moving towards the Palace.

She was now seeing the peril she had sensed within herself and she recognised that she must do something.

Running across her bedroom, just as she was in her nightgown, she opened the door.

The Count and Prince Vaslov had been given State rooms without any argument and they were on the opposite side of the corridor to hers and Udele's.

The nearest, Zoleka knew, was Prince Vaslov's.

She ran across towards his door, opened it without knocking and went in.

The room was dark as on this side of the Palace no moonlight filtered in from the sides of the curtains.

But she could just make out in the total blackness that Prince Vaslov was asleep in a large four-poster bed.

She ran to the side of it.

"Wake up!" she called. "Wake up quickly! There is danger."

With the alertness of a soldier he woke at once.

"What is it?" he asked.

"There are a number of strangers moving through the bushes towards the other side of the Palace. I can see them from my window."

Prince Vaslov sat up in bed.

"Go and wake Franz, while I get dressed."

Zoleka did as she was told.

She rushed from the room, down the corridor and into the room occupied by the Count.

He woke as quickly as the Prince had done.

"It is what I expected," he muttered. "Tell Prince Vaslov to operate his alarm. I will look after Udele."

Without waiting to hear any more, Zoleka did what he had asked.

She left his room and ran back to the corridor again.

There she saw Prince Vaslov, wearing his shirt and trousers and carrying a large object in one hand, going into her bedroom.

She hurried after him.

"The Count," she whispered, "said you are to use your alarm."

"That is exactly what I am going to do."

He went to the window and Zoleka followed him.

He pulled aside the curtain and looked out and she did the same.

Now there was no movement in the bushes where she had seen it before.

The leaves were all still in the bright moonlight, but there was a definite movement a little further away beneath some trees and behind a large flower bed.

Prince Vaslov stood looking out into the garden and Zoleka saw him lift up what he was carrying in his hand.

He threw it out of the window up into the air and as he did so, it exploded, making a loud noise in the silence.

At the same time it emitted a brilliant light.

It was so unexpected that Zoleka gave a cry and he put out his arm and pulled her against him.

"It is all right, my darling," he told her. "It will not hurt you, but it will bring help. Go and hide yourself by the bed."

The endearment he had used made Zoleka look up at him in astonishment.

And next she felt his lips touch hers gently before he pushed her away.

As she crouched down beside the bed, she saw him draw a revolver from his belt.

CHAPTER SEVEN

There was silence.

As Zoleka felt she must see what was happening in the garden, she rushed back to stand beside Prince Vaslov.

He glanced down at her with a faint smile.

He was closely watching, she was aware, the wing of the Palace – the wing where Prince Majmir's apartments were situated.

She dared not speak.

Then suddenly the Prince bent forward and fired his revolver.

Not, as she had expected, towards the wing of the Palace, but straight in front of him.

Now she could see several men coming through the trees and bushes at the far end of the garden.

They were moving quickly and silently, which had something sinister about it.

She was convinced that they were Prussians.

As the explosion of the Prince's revolver rang out, the men in front hesitated.

Then there was firing from every side of the garden and Zoleka knew that it was from Prince Vaslov's soldiers.

The noise seemed to echo and re-echo around the Palace and was almost deafening.

She had the idea, although it was so difficult to see, that although the Prussians were carrying guns, they were slow in using them.

Suddenly and almost as quickly as it had all started, the firing ceased.

Zoleka could see that there were bodies lying on the ground beyond the fountain.

She looked to the right and there were a number of men sprawled just outside a door leading into the Palace.

Prince Vaslov waited for a minute just in case there was any more firing and then he put his revolver back into his belt.

"I must find Franz and go down to the garden with him to see what has happened."

He put his arm round Zoleka.

"You have been superb, my dearest, as I knew you would be."

He kissed her forehead.

Then as if he was forcing himself to press on with the business waiting for him, he strode from the room.

Zoleka reckoned that the Count was with Udele so she followed him.

It was only a few steps to the door to Udele's room and it was ajar.

Prince Vaslov opened it and they were both about to walk in when they stopped.

At the far end of the room, silhouetted against the window, the Count held Udele closely in his arms and was kissing her fervently.

Prince Vaslov stiffened for a moment and stared as if this was something he had not expected.

He quietly closed the door and put his arms around Zoleka.

"If that," he murmured, "is how the wind blows, it certainly suits me. *Now*, my darling, I am free to tell you how much I love you."

His lips were on hers.

Almost before she realised what was happening to her, he was kissing her demandingly and passionately as if he would never let her go.

It was sublime, it was glorious, it was unbelievable.

She felt as if the whole Palace was turning topsy-turvy over her head.

She was flying up to the stars.

"I love you, I adore you, Zoleka," Prince Vaslov breathed in a deep and rather unsteady voice. "But now I really must go and find out what has happened."

He was about to turn away when the Count opened the door.

"Oh, there you are, Vaslov," he called. "I think we ought to go down and clear up the mess."

"I agree with you, Franz, but the girls are to stay up here."

"Of course."

Udele had followed the Count across the room and now she asked in a trembling voice,

"Do you think many of our men are dead?"

"I shall be surprised if there are any. You are not to worry about it. We will tell you and Zoleka all about it in the morning."

The Count hurried after Prince Vaslov who already was walking towards the stairs.

Udele put out her hand towards Zoleka.

"Will we be safe?" she asked her in a whisper.

"I don't think there is anyone left to harm us. Now we must do as they have told us. We must go to bed and try to sleep as there is sure to be an enormous amount for us to do tomorrow."

"You are quite sure that Franz will be safe?"

Zoleka realised it was difficult for Udele to think of anything except the man she loved.

"I am quite certain," she told her quietly, "that both of them will be safe, now come along with me. There is plenty of room in my bed for both of us."

"Oh, can I? I am so frightened of being alone."

"Don't worry so, we will be together and we can lie quietly in bed and think how lucky we are to have two such wonderful men to protect us."

She nearly added, " – and to love us."

Then she thought perhaps it was too soon to talk to Udele about the Count.

It had somehow never entered Zoleka's head that he might fall in love with her – even though it was to be expected that Udele would love him.

After all she had seen very few men and the Count was most attractive.

Zoleka was a little afraid at the back of her mind that perhaps he had been kissing Udele just to comfort her because she was so frightened and that he had no serious intentions where she was concerned.

Then she told herself it would be very difficult for him not to love anyone as beautiful and unspoilt as Udele.

She had been aware that Udele was wildly attracted by him – even if she did not understand that it was love.

They went into Zoleka's room and after she had lit some candles and pulled the curtains over the window they both climbed into bed.

Zoleka knew that Udele was thinking of the Count and praying that he would be safe – it was just what she herself wanted to do for Prince Vaslov.

She was still worried that despite what he had said and the sheer wonder of his kisses, they would not be able to be married.

Yet Krnov could be saved just as effectively by the Count as by Prince Vaslov.

'I would *love* to be his wife. I want to be with him for ever and always,' murmured Zoleka to herself.

She was saying it over and over again until she fell asleep.

*

They were awoken in the morning by Marla pulling back the curtains.

When Udele sat up in bed, Marla announced,

"It's nearly nine o'clock, Your Royal Highnesses, and I've been told to inform you that your breakfast will be served in the boudoir and Your Royal Highnesses are not to go down stairs until you're asked to do so."

Both of them were well aware that this order could only have come from Prince Vaslov.

They dare not disobey it, so they got up, dressed in their prettiest clothes and took their breakfast alone in the boudoir.

"I wonder what is happening," Udele kept saying. "I cannot think why no one comes and tells us."

"We shall know everything in due course," Zoleka told her soothingly. "I am quite certain there is a great deal to be sorted out downstairs. And that it is not for your eyes or mine."

She was thinking of the dead bodies being removed from the garden.

She had the idea that the Prussians who had entered the Palace might have killed some of the Krnovian guards in doing so.

She was to learn two hours later that she was right.

Both Princesses were feeling nervous and on edge and it was an overpowering relief when an equerry finally came to the boudoir.

"His Royal Highness, Prince Vaslov," he intoned, "would be most obliged if Your Royal Highnesses would join him in the Blue drawing room."

They sprang immediately to their feet and followed the equerry who moved rather slowly down the stairs.

Zoleka knew that Udele was longing to run ahead and find the Count.

Both Prince Vaslov and the Count were waiting for them in the Blue drawing room and to Zoleka's relief there was no one else present.

She walked slowly towards Prince Vaslov who was smiling at her.

Udele, however, gave a cry of joy.

Running to the Count, she flung herself at once into his arms.

"You are safe! You are safe!" she cried. "I was so frightened that something terrible had happened to you."

"Nothing has happened to me, my dearest darling," the Count answered, "except that I have been a long time without you!"

Udele looked up at him.

There was so much love in her eyes that the Count, as if he could not help himself, kissed her gently.

Then he said,

"Come and sit down. Prince Vaslov has a lot to tell us and we do not have much time."

Zoleka wanted to ask, " – much time for what?"

Prince Vaslov led her to a sofa and as she sat down, he stood in front of the mantelpiece.

"Firstly," he began, "I want to thank both of you for being so extremely sensible last night and behaving exactly as you should do in what was a very difficult situation."

"What happened last night?" asked Zoleka.

"What Franz and I had anticipated. The Prussians, when they saw my soldiers arriving, realised they had no chance of taking over the City as they had intended."

"So they did intend to do so!" exclaimed Zoleka.

"Of course they did. They had just mobilised quite a number of troops on the border, but not enough even with those who had already infiltrated into the City to be certain of victory against my soldiers."

Zoleka gave a sigh of relief.

"They knew that the only chance they now had of gaining control of Krnov was to kidnap the ruling Prince and make him abdicate at the point of a pistol."

Udele gave a cry of horror and the Count put his arm round her.

"Have they taken Papa?" she asked in a trembling voice.

"That is what they intended to do, but fortunately Zoleka spied them creeping through the Palace gardens. I must admit they came quicker and sooner than either Franz or I had expected."

"Did they reach Papa?" enquired Udele nervously.

"They reached your father, but were not rough with him as they wanted to take him alive. However, when they were carrying him, because he is not able to walk, through the door into the garden, the firing started. So they threw him down on the ground and ran away."

Udele gave a sigh of relief.

"So Papa is alive and well?"

"He is alive," Prince Vaslov answered her, "but I am very sorry to tell you that he has suffered a stroke. He is now unconscious but in no pain and the doctors are with him."

"I am so glad he is not dead," whispered Udele.

"I too am very glad that he did not die at the hands of our enemies. But you have to be very brave and face the fact that it is unlikely that he will live very long. Therefore it is extremely important that you should agree to do what we want you to do."

"What is that?"

"To save this country, which is what I came here to achieve, it is absolutely essential that the people of Krnov should immediately acquire a Ruler, who they will respect and of whom our enemies will be afraid."

Now both Udele and Zoleka were staring at Prince Vaslov questioningly.

It flashed through Zoleka's mind that maybe he was going to replace Udele with someone else.

She could not think of who it could possibly be if it was not himself.

Because he could read her thoughts, Prince Vaslov smiled at her before he said softly,

"No, you are quite wrong!"

Raising his voice, he now addressed Udele,

"What I do advise and Franz agrees with me, is that you and he should be married immediately. It is the only way our enemies will recognise there is a man in charge as well as a beautiful Princess and they now have no possible chance of taking over Krnov as they intended to do."

Udele turned to look at the Count, who put his arm round her and drew her close to him.

"I have every intention, my beautiful Princess," he

murmured "of marrying you, but it does mean the Marriage Service must take place tomorrow!"

"But that is the day of our ball."

The Count laughed.

"What could be a more perfect way to celebrate our marriage than to dance the night away with all our friends instead of having the usual rather boring reception?"

Udele gave a little laugh.

"It would certainly be something new."

"That is the right word. Everything in this country is going to be new when you and I rule it together."

"I think perhaps this is the right moment," Prince Vaslov came in, "to tell Udele that she is not marrying, as she believes, a very charming and handsome young Count, but someone far more significant."

"What are you saying to me?" asked Udele. "I do not understand."

"Zoleka invited Franz to come to Krnov with her, because she knew that he would help her make the Palace a genuine Royal Residence as it should have been under her father's rule."

He paused for a moment.

"Instead it has become dingy, dilapidated and dull. Whatever else has happened, you must see there is already a vast improvement since Franz and Zoleka arrived."

"They have been fantastic in everything they have done," agreed Udele. "But tell me why is Franz so grand?"

"He is the grandson of the Emperor of Austria and his own father, the Archduke, is one of the most influential grandees in Vienna."

Udele gasped and turned to look at the man beside her.

"Whether I am a Count or a Prince, my darling," he said, "I adore you and it is going to be very challenging for me to try to make this country worthy of your beauty. I have a feeling that, with all the entertainment Vaslov has arranged, the people are already thinking we have changed what was almost a pigsty into a Fairyland!"

"That is exactly what *you* are doing," cried Udele. "And if you are so grand, I am marrying a 'Fair Prince'."

"And if you are marrying him tomorrow," Zoleka pointed out, "it is going to be rush, rush, rush to find you a wedding gown."

Udele gave a cry.

"Oh, I must have one! I must look pretty for Franz and of course for the people who will be watching us."

"I have already sent for the Archbishop of Krnov," Prince Vaslov added, "and Anton Bauer has gone to see the Prime Minister to tell him about all that has happened and to inform him of your impending marriage."

"I knew Franz loved me when he kissed me," Udele confessed shyly, "but he has not actually yet asked me to marry him."

"That is most remiss of me," the Count responded. "I will ask you when we are alone, so that I can kiss you after every word!"

Udele gave a giggle and smiled up at him.

"I would love that," she whispered.

They were obviously so happy together that Zoleka looked up at Prince Vaslov.

There was a question in her eyes and he said as if she had asked it aloud,

"Once they are safely married and we have enjoyed their ball, you and I will go back to your father. I know you will wish to be married in your own country and then, my lovely one, we will have a quiet honeymoon after all this rush and tumble when I can tell you how much I love and adore you."

"That is just what I want to hear,"

The Prince gave a deep sigh before he added,

"I thought I would never be married at all because I would never find anyone like you. But the moment I saw you I just knew that you were the one woman in the world I wanted as my wife."

There was such a special note in his voice that told Zoleka without words that he had suffered an intolerable agony.

He had sincerely believed that he must sacrifice his own desires and think only of saving Krnov.

And incidentally his own country and Opava.

It seemed so incredible that everything should have worked out so perfectly.

Zoleka put her hand on his arm as she sighed,

"We have been so very very lucky.

"Very lucky indeed, my darling."

As he spoke Udele and Franz rose and walked to the other end of the drawing room.

They were obviously saying private words to each other and did not wish to be overheard.

The Prince looked at them before saying to Zoleka,

"You do fully appreciate that the doctors say Prince Majmir cannot live long. It is thus essential that Udele is married tomorrow and then the whole world will know that Franz will rule Krnov with all the might and importance of the State of Austria behind him."

"Of course I understand and I know too that Udele will be very happy."

"She will do everything he asks her and I think, like me, he is very grateful to God for sending him a woman who loves him for himself and not for his position."

Zoleka laughed.

"She thought that he was only a Count, and it will be delightful for her when he takes her to Vienna to meet his family."

"Of course it will, but I am not worried about them any longer. Find her a wedding gown and let them enjoy their ball. After that I want you *all* to myself."

Zoleka smiled at him.

"That is what I want too."

Her voice was almost a whisper as she added,

"I have prayed and prayed so often that some day I would find love – the real love that my father and mother had for each other. When you walked across the garden towards me, you answered all my prayers."

"Did you think you would be able to marry me?"

Zoleka shook her head.

"When I finally admitted to myself that I loved you, I thought it was just completely hopeless as you wanted to marry Udele. I knew I would never love anyone else and there would never be another man in my life."

She knew the Prince was very moved by what she was saying.

He looked down at her eyes and sighed,

"I only wish that it was you and I who were being married tomorrow. But my precious, beautiful Goddess, I cannot wait very long."

"We will arrange our wedding as soon as we get back to Papa. I know how pleased he will be as he admires you so much for all you have done for your country."

"And I greatly admire him too," he insisted. "So we must try hard not to make him feel too lonely because I have taken you away from him."

"Only you could be so kind and understanding. Oh, Vaslov, I love you so much that it is very difficult to think of anything else."

"I will tell you just how much I love you, my dear darling Zoleka, the night we are married."

They looked into each other's eyes.

Through the mercy of God Himself the impossible had become the possible and the unbelievable had become credible.

They were both convinced in their hearts that they had been searching for each other through many lives and their love was so incredibly strong and unbreakable that it would last through many more lives yet to come.

For them this was the Love they had always sought.

It came from God, was part of God, and would be theirs for all Eternity.